Realms of Fire & Shadow

Fae Witch Chronicles Book 3

J. S. Malcom

ISBN-13:978-1981139507
ISBN-10:1981139508

CHAPTER 1

Moments ago, I was chilly and pulling my hood up against the rain. Now, as I walk beside Cade, the stars shine above and a mild breeze caresses my face. Both would be pleasant enough, except the sudden shift in atmosphere only serves to remind me that I've once again entered a different realm. One not truly meant for humans, and with just a misty bridge separating me from that other realm I so narrowly escaped.

I knew I'd be back, of course. At least to Faerie, if not Silvermist. There's never been a choice. I couldn't possibly forget that Julia remains trapped, nor could I forget the unspoken promise I made to Helen, Lily and Mitch. These were never options. Still, I'd be lying to myself not to admit that I've remained terrified at the thought of returning. More frightened than I've ever felt at the prospect of facing vampires, demons or even body snatchers. Those creatures, I've faced on my terms, in my own realm, where my powers as a veil witch have afforded me a level playing field. Like last time, I have no idea what to expect from what lies ahead. I only know it can't be good.

Still, first things first, and I turn to Cade. "What have you heard? Where's Julia?"

Cade nods as we keep walking, obviously not surprised to be getting right down to business. "At the palace. At least, we're pretty sure."

I've been back in Silvermist for mere minutes and already my mind teems with questions. "Who's *we*?" I say. "How can you be sure? Hang on, there's a palace?"

Cade glances over, shrugging to underscore what he says next. "It's kind of a long story. I should probably just start at the beginning."

"Okay. Sorry." I glance up as a meteor streaks across the sky, blazing bright and tinged with hues of orange and green. It's the second I've seen since we've been walking, and I'm curious, but it will have to wait.

"Don't be sorry," Cade says. "I get it. The whole mess is confusing as hell. Okay, so after it happened, you know, that thing in the alley—"

He only gets that far before I interrupt him again. "What the hell was that? Did you know that could happen?"

"Well, technically, yes." Cade rubs the back of his neck, possibly due to stress, or maybe because his head still hurts from when those guys knocked him out with a club.

After a week of concern for him, and a million times hoping he wasn't dead, I'm suddenly pissed off. I can't help it. "Do you think you should have mentioned that? Do you have any idea what I went through?"

Cade winces. "Kind of. Not all of it. Sorry."

I shake my head in disbelief. "*Sorry?*"

"Well, I mean, that sort of thing doesn't usually happen in Gorgedden. Usually, we're safe there. Relatively speaking, of course."

I narrow my eyes. "Of course."

"Well, what I mean is, that's more the kind of thing you'd expect if you wandered into Seelie territory. Those guys must have been getting paid a lot to take a risk like that. As you can imagine, the Unseelie don't take kindly to anyone caught trafficking captives to the Seelie."

This time I scowl at him. "Great. I'll take comfort in knowing that."

"Honestly. I should just start at the beginning."

I try to ignore another meteor, this one tinged blue and yellow. "Okay sure. Please start at the beginning."

We turn a corner onto the main street running through Silvermist, or at least the part of it I've seen before. Light spills from the windows of businesses as people walk along in pairs and groups. A few ride slowly by on horses. None seem worried, or in any particular rush.

Cade too looks around, as if distracted. "Where to begin?" he says.

I grit my teeth. "At the beginning."

Despite the edge to my voice, he laughs. "Right, sorry. The beginning. Let's see if we can make that happen." He takes a deep breath, and then exhales. "Okay, so that thing happened in the alley. One of those guys sapped me, and when I woke up you were gone. Don't get me wrong. I totally freaked out but, to be honest, part of me felt pretty sure you'd be okay. I mean, if you're the one from the

3

proph—" Cade clears his throat. "Never mind. We'll get to that later."

My non-pointy ears definitely prick up at that one, but I decide to hear Cade out.

"The only thing I could think of was that we told Revlen we'd meet her in the morning. Remember her?"

I do, of course. "The rebel cell leader."

Cade looks around. "I know we're not in Faerie, but you might want to keep it down. Anyway, yeah, her. Remember that guy Ecubon she mentioned? Well, he showed up as promised and Revlen asked him about your friend. Turns out he saw a girl matching her description being taken through town about two weeks ago."

Those images from before rise within my mind again—captives tied to horses, terrified and humiliated as they're paraded through town.

"I'm sorry," Cade says. "I know this can't be easy to hear. But, hopefully, she's okay. Your friend, Julia. See, here's the thing—Ecubon said she was brought in by Vintain himself. He got word that she was taken to the palace. So, what I'm thinking is that she must be considered valuable. Otherwise, she wouldn't be there."

Two things click into place for me. The first is that I've heard that name before. Vintain. Raakel's husband mentioned that he and his men were the ones looking for me. The other is that Cade must be right. Julia is valuable, because she's bait.

"Vintain," I say under my breath, committing his name to memory this time.

4

Cade assumes I'm speaking to him. "Right, Vintain. High Mage, advisor to the Queen. Tall bastard, so pale he's nearly albino. He rides out sometimes with the Royal Guard to intimidate the lowly masses. You might remember him from when we ran for our lives and hid in the sewer."

So that's Vintain. I do remember him, of course. I'll never forget that scene, when the fanfare sounded and those men rode in on their horses, their leader targeting that couple for humiliation. I never saw his face, but I remember the way the hairs rose on the back of my neck, and that undeniable sense of familiarity.

In my heart I know, but I ask just to be sure. "Does he have a scar?"

"Down the side of his face," Cade says. "Ironic, isn't it? The Seelie are vain as hell, but all the magic in the world won't take a scar like that away, because magic put it there. At least, that's the story. Some other mage did that to him."

"That was Grayson." Again, I say it more to myself than to Cade.

Cade touches me on the shoulder. "Are you okay?"

The real answer is, *Not really. Not at all.* My blood boils at just the thought of him, and what he did to Julia. Not to mention Lauren Flannery, and who could guess how many more.

But what I say is, "I'm fine."

"Okay, good. I'm sure you've been through a lot. But, yeah, I've been thinking it had to be him. Especially given the level of magic you described. They can do a lot using changelings, but full-on magic? Teleportation? That's a far cry from run of the mill spying and creeping about. To channel that kind of power, you'd have to be a mage."

Which, come to think of it, has to be the only thing Grayson wasn't lying about. No, not Grayson. He was the old man who toppled over dead in a doorway, his life stolen. The man I knew—the *creature* I knew—is called Vintain.

Once again, I consider this ability of the fae—at least the Seelie fae—to exist in our world using changelings. Given the extent of what they appear capable of experiencing in that form, I have to wonder why they ever bothered inhabiting our realm physically. Greed, I guess. Power. That seems to be what they're about.

"Unfortunately, by the time I found out about your friend, you were already gone," Cade says, snapping me out of my reverie. "Revlen's people had no idea who those guys were who abducted you, nor where you might have ended up. So, I was pretty much stuck."

I almost interrupt him again to say, *You were stuck?* But I decide to let it slide.

"I spent a couple days searching for you," Cade says. "I didn't have any luck, obviously. After that, I kept hopping back and forth between the human realm and Faerie. I figured, if you escaped, you probably wouldn't come back to Silvermist. I mean, I guess you could have if you'd wanted to, but it didn't seem likely. Besides, I knew Isaac and Sloane would step in if you showed up. Anyway, I was right. You went back home, and here we are again."

I see the oval wooden sign for the Rowan and Thistle hanging above the sidewalk up ahead, so I guess that must be where we're heading.

"Speaking of which," I say. "Why *are* we here? Wouldn't it make more sense to be in Faerie?" A chill ripples down my spine just thinking about the place, enough so that I shudder.

"First, because you have to be careful where and when you enter Faerie," Cade says. "Things have been heating up fast over there. Also, I should probably check in with Isaac and Sloane, not to mention Hellhound."

That one gets a double-take. "You haven't checked on your dog in two weeks?"

We stop outside the door to the bar. "Technically, Hellhound isn't my dog. I'm more his adopted half-human. Besides, Isaac and Sloane look after him too. They pretty much have to, the big mooch."

We enter the tavern, and as we cross through the room I don't look to see if people stare at me. I've got bigger fish to fry than to worry about whether I'm giving off an outsider vibe. Desdemona, on the other hand, I can't help but notice, since she's already staring daggers my way. Damn, that pixie doesn't miss a trick, and apparently she's a champion at holding a grudge.

We claim a couple of barstools and Melanie nods from where she stands at the beer taps filling a couple of mugs, to let us know she sees us.

"Where was I?" Cade says.

I try to think back through his scattered narrative. "You kept going back and forth between realms."

Cade nods. "Oh, right. That's how I found out about—"

"How are you guys tonight?"

Melanie wipes down the bar while Desdemona spins a couple of coasters out in front of us. Naturally, she glares at me. I swear, if Jerome and Bobby ever drag her back to the Cauldron again, I will seriously kick their asses.

"Pretty good," Cade says. "A pint of Oberon for me, please."

Melanie turns her attention to me. "So, you came back."

It's hard to say how she feels about that, but I just say, "Couldn't stay away."

She cracks a smile. "Yeah, that's pretty much how it works. Once you know it's here, Silvermist can be pretty addictive."

Yeah, it's a great place, other than it being a gateway to Hell. I do my best to scrounge up a smile too. "I guess I'll have an Oberon too, please."

Because how could we possibly set out to save my best friend without stopping off first for a beer? I'm starting to wonder if Cade might be both a thief and a lush. Although, maybe he needs to keep himself partly numb to stay sane. I can't really blame him, considering how much crazy shit he seems to deal with on a regular basis.

Melanie goes to get our beers, Desdemona flips me off, and I turn to Cade before we lose the thread again. "That's how you found out..." I look at him expectantly.

For a moment, Cade stares at me blankly. Then he makes the connection. "Oh, right. That's how I found out that you freed a freaking changeling!" Heads turn at his sudden outburst, and he lowers his voice again. "You realize that's never happened before, right?"

I shrug. "Beginner's luck, I guess."

Cade stares at me for a moment, as if waiting for me to say more. When I don't, he continues. "Somehow word got out about it too. Revlen said Lady Ferntree, or whatever the hell her name is, was totally freaking out. Of course she was. She not only lost two slaves—she also let a fugitive slip right through her fingers. On top of that, you made her husband look like a total fool. There Vintain was looking all over the place for you, and you were right there under his nose the entire time."

It's not news to me that I was being searched for, although the reminder doesn't exactly improve my mood, considering where we're going. All the same, I use it to segue back to Julia.

"So, Vintain. Does he live at the palace?"

Cade sips his beer and nods. "He's part of the court, definitely."

"And I suppose there must be a king and queen, and all that?"

"Just a queen," Cade says. "High Queen Abarrane."

I slug back more of my own beer, disgusted. "High Queen Abarrane? Isn't that a bit redundant?"

Cade laughs. "Right, there's no low queen. In fact, there aren't any other queens at all. Not since the Winter Court prevailed in the war for magic."

Why doesn't this surprise me? "Let me guess, a war fought with magic to see who got control of the magic."

A smile tugs at Cade's lips. "I see you're getting the picture. The Seelie definitely lack a sense of irony."

I heave out a sigh. "Irony is a difficult sensibility to manage when your entire existence centers on self-importance."

Despite my tone, Cade laughs. "Exactly. Apparently, you've already mastered the subject of Seelie nobility. That was fast."

Cade raises his mug and I clink mine against his, although I'm not sure what we're drinking to. Absurdity? Futility? Desperation and hatred? Take your pick.

"I had something of a crash course," I remind him. "Thankfully, I was able to graduate within a week. And by graduate, I mean barely escape with my life. Which reminds me, what was that thing you said before? Well, that thing you almost said. I could have sworn you were about to say *prophecy*, but I'm sure I must have gotten that part wrong."

Cade lifts his eyebrows as he hesitates, but then says, "Don't freak out or anything. I've been trying to find a way to tell you for a while now."

Desdemona, I notice, is hovering a bit too close for my comfort. So, she's a nosy little creature too. I narrow my eyes at her and she flitters back over to where Melanie is talking to some customers. I turn back to Cade again. "Why do I get the feeling I'm not going to like this part?"

Not that there's been a part I've actually liked so far.

Cade lowers his voice. "To be honest, until now I haven't been sure. Although, like I said, if it was true, I figured you weren't likely to end up spending the rest of your life as Lady Fernpot's kitchen bitch. But then you managed to achieve the impossible."

He stares at me intently, as if waiting for me to say something. "Are we talking about freeing Ellie again? Because obviously that wasn't impossible. I did it."

Cade nods emphatically. "My point entirely. For anyone else, in the history of Faerie, reversing one of their changeling spells has been impossible. Apparently, that doesn't apply to you."

Despite the fact that half the time I can barely take Cade seriously, I feel my pulse start to escalate. He's having a hard time getting to the point, for one thing. He also started by telling me not to freak out. In my experience, whenever someone tells you not to freak out, it's time to do just that.

"Cade, what are you trying to tell me?"

Cade drains the last of his beer, glances at Melanie, and digs in his pocket. He comes up with a pair of jeweled earrings and a swiveling glass eye. He sets the glass eye on the bar and shoves the earrings back into his pocket. "Maybe it would be better if I showed you. Come on. There's someone I'd like you to meet."

CHAPTER 2

I wait until we get outside to say anything. Mostly because I wanted to be sure Melanie wasn't about to sic her enforcer pixie on us again. She was watching Cade carefully and, as soon as he set that glass eye down, the thing started swiveling on top of the bar as if it was looking around the room. Payment was sufficient, apparently, since we left without incident. So, the price of two pints of Oberon Amber in Silvermist is equal to, or less than, the value of a magical glass eye. My knowledge base keeps expanding every day.

The other reason I didn't say anything was because I wasn't sure if I might start yelling. I don't exactly speak softly now. "*Seriously?* You're going to go all mysterious on me after that?"

Cade glances over as we start walking, giving me that nerdy smile. He really is kind of cute with his curly hair and the points of his ears shining pale in the moonlight. Not like I want to jump his bones cute. More like friend cute, or little brother cute. That is, if I had a little brother who so happened to be a half-human, half-fae thief of magical objects with an obvious penchant for amber ale and a death wish.

"I'm not going for dramatic effect," he says. "And besides, Kezia doesn't live far from here."

"Who's Kezia?"

"Kezia Grinsly," Cade says. "Don't worry. You'll like her."

As if that's not deliberately slathering on more mystery. I'm thinking about punching him in the face when a streak of light shoots across the sky, followed by another.

I point up to the stars. "That's one heck of a meteor shower. Have you even noticed?"

Cade glances up, and then nods. "Yeah, I've noticed, but I keep hoping it will stop. That's no meteor shower. The same deal is going on in Faerie, only way more intense. It started five days ago."

Five days ago. That's right after I escaped. "What's the deal?"

"I'm guessing it has to be some sort of magical side-effect. The magic's gone totally unstable in Faerie and it's screwing with everything. They've been getting fireballs, earthquakes, freak lightning storms. All kinds of craziness. Now, it's starting to happen here."

I shake my head, trying to make sense of what he just said. I get the part about the misuse of magic messing with Faerie's environment. I've experienced it first-hand with the snow that isn't snow, along with the somehow frozen glittering magical fallout. Sure, it's seriously weird, but no weirder than demons who can exploit your deepest fears or entities that can eject your spirit from your body. It's not always a matter of what's supposed to be, as much as a matter of what's supposed to be where. It wouldn't surprise me if in some realms there are lakes that talk and birds

13

performing microsurgery with their beaks. Weird is all relative to your perspective. But I'm not sure how magical instability in one realm can cause the same in another.

Maybe it's my lack of response, or that Cade just reads me once again. I'd almost forgotten, but he's good at guessing what's on my mind. "Another quick interdimensional physics lecture, brought to you by me," he says. "Although, this one is largely speculative."

I try not to sigh. "And the last one about energy vortexes was grounded in empirical fact?"

Cade laughs. "Undoubtedly, somewhere. As I was saying."

He glances over at me and I have to laugh too. I might as well enjoy myself while I still can. "As you were saying, professor."

"It's simple, really. All the realms are interconnected, so anything affecting one affects all. Maybe in small ways, in some places, while in others the impact is felt more dramatically. What we know for sure is that the magical wellspring is being run dry in Faerie, so seriously bad stuff is happening there, both socially and environmentally. It's all about balance, so it's no wonder the place is a total mess. Imagine that same magic as a source feeding all the connected realms. For different reasons, maybe, but still playing a significant role of some nature." He points to the sky as another star appears to fall. "Mess with it bad enough and, voila. At least some aspects of that imbalance start to manifest elsewhere. Makes perfect sense when you think about it."

And it does, in a very weird way. It's not something I would have thought of before. It's not something I *could* have thought of before, but to say my perspective has changed recently would be the understatement of the century.

"Still with me?" Cade says.

"Absolutely. What's that about?"

I point down the road to where several fires glow and a crowd, mostly cast in silhouette, can be seen milling about. As we get closer, voices rise into the night. The loudest is that of a woman, her shadowy form raised above the crowd, suggesting that she must be standing on something. It's the first time I've heard true anger in Silvermist.

"We just can't turn a blind eye to this any longer!" she cries out. "We've ignored the oppression of our Unseelie brothers and sisters for far too long. And now we're paying the price!"

As if to deliberately emphasize her point, fiery lights shoot through the night sky above us, first one and then two more.

"Hey, it's not our fight or our problem!" a man calls back. "And I don't live in Faerie!"

A woman calls out from somewhere else in the crowd. "He's right! We come here to be left alone, because we don't belong in either world. Not the human realm, and definitely not the fae!"

More voices call out their support for this position, while others counter with cries of, "We have to help them!" and "It's our realm too!" Honestly, I can see both points of view. On one hand, why should these accidental children of Faerie give a damn what takes place within that realm? On the other hand, even if the struggle between the Seelie and Unseelie doesn't concern them, the magical imbalance is beginning to destabilize Silvermist. Add to that, what that one person called out is true. In a way, Faerie is their realm too, which is something I haven't really thought about before. After all, the only thing stopping them from going there is the threat of danger. Then again, for some reason I can go there too. Where does that put me in all of this?

The woman standing before the crowd holds out her hands, asking for quiet. "Please, listen to me! At least think about what I have to say. Like you, I didn't ask to grow up confused about what I was. I always felt different, and I didn't understand why. My own mother knew the truth, but she was too ashamed to tell me!"

In response, someone yells, "Exactly, and she shouldn't have had to feel that way. The shame is on the fae!" Someone else calls out, "To hell with the fae, and I mean all of them! When did the Unseelie ever stick up for us?"

Suddenly, another voice takes over, that of an old woman who has what sounds like a Russian accent. As she speaks, I crane to see her. I know her voice.

"We all know lore of this realm, yes? It come to us like magic itself, in our dreams and thoughts, like friend whisper in our ears. This voice part of Silvermist. It be spirit maybe, yes?"

The crowd grows still, all heads turning toward the old woman's voice as if they too have heard her speak before.

"The lore say time will come when choice must be made. That we see signs when that time come. Place suddenly start to change, no longer be the same. You know this, yes?"

To my surprise, people nod and murmur their agreement. I keep trying to see the woman who's speaking, but I'm too short to see past the people blocking my view.

"Lore says one of those signs be that stranger come here. And this stranger have power within her to help. You heard this, yes?"

Again, people nod, a few saying, "Yes," to let the woman know she's not wrong. Suddenly, those standing in front of me shift and I can finally see past them. At the front of the crowd, the old woman stands beside a fire burning in a barrel. So much has happened since, that I completely forgot about the old woman who forced a psychic reading upon me at the Saturday Market. But I realize now that's who's been speaking. I remember now; Cade said her name was Eva.

As if she knows I'm there, and knew all along, Eva stares at me for a silent moment. Then she says, "This stranger not know what she is, or why she come here. But soon she find out."

Cade starts walking and I follow after him, tearing my eyes away from Eva and the scene around us, as Eva's words from before echo within my mind.

Fae witch! You see, Cassie. Fae witch!

Cade must have missed that moment of eye contact between me and Eva, because he just says, "Feels different here, doesn't it?"

And he's right, it does. I've only visited Silvermist once before, but on this same street last time people walked as couples holding hands, or as groups talking and laughing. Now, the fear and confusion is evident as people stand in crowds arguing and debating. It seems clear that the two realms are very much in flux, and I have to wonder when these changes will make themselves known in the realm I call my own.

CHAPTER 3

It isn't long before we walk along a mostly empty cobblestone street. As in the rest of Silvermist, gas jet streetlamps light our way, but the large stone houses around us, with ivy clinging to their fronts, feel older and more Gothic than the other structures I've seen here.

"This part of town was settled a while ago, to say the least," Cade says. "Although, it's far from being the oldest part of Silvermist. As you can imagine, people have been finding their way here for a long time. Basically since the fae started mixing with humans."

Given that the fae have been part of human legend for a very long time, it's hard to imagine what the oldest parts of town might hold. Castles of roughly hewn stone? Thatch huts? Tents made of fur?

Cade looks around at the houses, as if he too isn't quite sure where we are. He stops and says, "I think it's that one over there. I forget. It's been like a million years."

It's only when he says it that it occurs to me. "This Kezia person, is she expecting us?"

"Not exactly," Cade says. "But the last time I saw her she said to drop in any time I felt like it."

"But you just said it's been a million years."

Cade changes his mind and starts walking again. "I can be a little hyperbolic sometimes. More like, I don't know, ten?"

"Hang on. You haven't seen Kezia in ten years and we're just going to knock on her front door?" I look around at the gloomy stone houses and add, "At night?"

"It's not that late. What is it, seven maybe? Seven-thirty?"

I pull my phone from my pocket to check, but it shows just a string of zeros where the time should be. Of course, since the nearest cell tower is basically on another planet.

Cade laughs. "I believe we covered that last time. Cell phones—"

"Don't work here," I say. "I know."

"Do you?" Cade asks merrily.

Asshole.

"Wait, I think it's that one."

Cade stops again and squints through the glowing mist that, come to think of it, seems thicker in this part of town. I wonder if that has anything to do with it being older.

"Yeah, that's it definitely," Cade says. "Can you read the numbers?"

I peer through the darkness at the front of the house. "Wait, you just said that's definitely it. Why am I looking for numbers?"

"There I go being hyperbolic again. I mean I'm pretty sure that's it."

"Gotcha. You're definitely pretty sure."

No wonder I got abducted. I put my life in the hands of a guy who steals from highly powerful magical beings, exaggerates all the time, and sucks back a pint of ale at every opportunity. Wait, aren't I putting my trust in him again? Why, yes I am, come to think of it.

My head snaps back to the house again, as a beam of light suddenly plays across the front of it. Then I realize that the light source is Cade's hand, and he's not holding a flashlight.

"Thirty-five-eleven," he says. "Yeah, I remember now."

The light winks out again as quickly as it appeared. Given how effortless that display of magic was, I have to wonder why I haven't seen more like it in this half-blood realm. At first I assumed it was the access to magic in Silvermist that brought people here, but clearly it's more about being with their own kind. Even at the gathering we just passed, magic didn't appear to be a central issue. Those present seemed most concerned about where they belonged.

Cade opens an iron gate and we follow a stone walk to the front door.

"Seriously, ten years?" I say.

"That's like yesterday in Silvermist." Cade knocks on the door. We wait, and when no one answers he uses the knocker this time.

From inside the house, I hear what sounds like a symphony blasting out the intro to Ride of the Valkyries. A coincidence? Apparently not, since it cuts off, but then repeats when Cade tries the knocker again. Nifty.

"Kezia always was creative with her use of magic," Cade says. "I kind of forgot that about her."

"Since yesterday?"

Cade ignores the comment.

A moment later, the front door opens and an old woman appears in the light spilling out of the house. She looks to be about seventy, small and thin, with pointy ears and gray hair pulled back into a bun. In her floral print dress, with reading glasses dangling from a faux-jeweled lanyard, she's simply adorable. She looks like an elf librarian.

She squints at Cade, then at me, and then back to Cade again. Her face lights up. "Cade, is that really you?"

"Hi Mrs. Grinsly," Cade says, immediately sounding like a ten-year-old. "I hope it's not too late."

She smiles warmly. "Not at all. Please come in."

We go inside and it's difficult to keep my jaw from dropping. The interior is stunning, the front hall alone featuring arched doorways leading toward other rooms, a high ceiling, crown molding with ornate plaster corbels, gleaming hardwood floors and gorgeous rugs. There's also a marble fireplace, something I've never seen in a front hall before, within which flames dance behind a screen shaped like a peacock. The walls are painted a pale shade of grayish blue. Damn, Kezia sure has nice taste. I hope she never sees my apartment.

Kezia smiles at me and then beams again at Cade. She sighs and says, "How long has it been? At least ten years, am I right?"

Cade's face starts to turn red and he refuses to look at me. "It feels like yesterday," he says.

Kezia looks him up and down, and then slips on her reading glasses to study his face. "Well, you've grown a lot. The last time I saw you, you couldn't have been more than fifteen."

"I think I was sixteen. Pretty sure, anyway."

Did we really just barge in unannounced on an old lady Cade hasn't seen since he was a kid? It's seems pretty bonked to me, but maybe it's okay in Silvermist. At least, Kezia doesn't seem worried about it.

She turns to me and says, "And who's this?"

Cade turns my way as well. "This is Cassie. Cassie, this is Mrs. Grinsly."

"Kezia, please," she says, shaking my hand. She turns to Cade and says, "And you too, young man. Since when did you start acting so formal? Now, let's go into the living room and find out what brings you here. I just made some tea. Would you like some?"

"We'd love some," Cade says. "Thank you."

We follow Kezia deeper into her house, which is amazing in every way. The living room features burgundy wallpaper with gold star shaped patterns, lush antique sofas and chairs, and a light blue ceiling where a beautiful brass light fixture descends from an ornate ceiling medallion. Kezia settles us on the sofa, goes off to get the tea, and returns a few minutes later bearing a tray.

"Can I help you?" I say, although I notice that Kezia doesn't seem to be having any issues handling things.

"I'm fine, dear. Thank you." She sets two china cups before us on the marble-topped coffee table—yet another exquisite piece of furniture—and takes the seat across from us.

Cade lifts his cup and blows at the steam. "Kezia has lived here since, when, the nineteen hundreds?"

Kezia nods, resting her cup and saucer on her thigh. "February of 1882, to be exact. At the time, this was considered to be the modern neighborhood. Can you imagine?"

"Your house is beautiful," I say.

Kezia's eyes gleam. "Thank you, dear. To be honest, I don't deserve much credit. Things don't age the same way in Silvermist."

That much seems evident, given that she's been living here for over 130 years. Cade mentioned that half-bloods can live a long time, but damn.

Kezia gestures to the walls. "For example, this is the original wallpaper. Strangely, it's only just lately that I've noticed it beginning to fade. I have my suspicions why that might be, but this isn't the time." She keeps her eyes on mine for a moment longer, and then says, "You're new here, aren't you?"

"Yes, I've only visited Silvermist twice now."

"Twice. I see." Kezia nods as she seems to consider something. "When was the first time?"

I hesitate, again wondering at the possible connection. It has to be a coincidence. "About two weeks ago."

Kezia nods. "I see."

Right, not long before things started going crazy here. But I can't imagine what that would have to do with me.

Kezia seems lost in thought for another few moments. Then she gestures toward Cade and offers him another soft smile. "Now this one, I met when he was little more than a boy. Not long after you first started coming over, as I recall."

"That's right," Cade says. "I was thirteen at the time."

"Thirteen." Kezia speaks softly, as if she can barely remember being that young. Which, I suppose, might very well be the case. She turns to me again. "Cade used to attend my lectures at the library. I still offer them once a week, to anyone interested in Silvermist history. As well as Faerie, as best I've been able to piece it together. Which, believe me, isn't easy to do, given how seldom we come across reliable resources. They can be difficult to procure. Can't they Cade?"

A smile passes between the two of them. Cade—my nerdy, thieving, hyperbolic friend—blushes bright red. You can't help but love the guy

In that moment, the back of my neck tingles as an image comes to me. I see a young version of Cade slipping across the bridge into Faerie, to bring back something valuable to a woman he admires. A mentor. A respected friend. How I know, I have no idea, but the image of a book flashes inside my mind. And somehow I also know that's where Cade got his start stealing from the Seelie.

"Getting certain artifacts can be problematic," Cade says.

Kezia narrows her eyes at him, even as her gaze gleams with fondness. "As in, bringing them back could easily get you killed. I certainly hope you've grown past that point in your life."

Cade hesitates. "I'm much more careful these days."

Kezia sips her tea. "I'm glad to hear that. So, what brings you two young people by this evening? I assume you weren't just out hunting for a good cup of tea. Although, if I do say so myself, I might well have perfected the art by now."

She says it just as I swallow my first sip, which tastes like herbal nirvana. What the hell is it with beverages in Silvermist?

"Well, now that you mention the library," Cade says. "Do you still keep some of your books here?"

A smile plays on Kezia's lips. "In fact, I do."

Cade looks at me. "Kezia is a bit of a bibliophile, just so you know. Kind of like your friend at Grimoire. What's her name again?"

Right, Cade had been spying on me for weeks before I met him. Amazingly, I've managed to move past the weird stalker part of our relationship. "Maggie," I say. I turn to Kezia and add, "She runs the bookstore where I work part time. She's pretty much devoted her life to rescuing obscure volumes."

"Well, I'd love to meet her," Kezia says. "Perhaps one of these days I will." She shifts her attention to Cade again. "Was there something here you were hoping to see?"

Cade nods. "Actually, it was one of the first items I brought back. Right after I started attending your lectures."

Apparently, Kezia makes the connection immediately. "The one that most certainly would have gotten you killed if you'd been caught."

"Well, they kill us if they can anyway," Cade says. "And I had a reasonably reliable tip that a certain monastery archive would soon need to be relocated. It seemed a chance worth taking."

"Which you can only say because you're still breathing." Kezia nods. "I still have it, of course. The Book of Temporal Projections. It remains where it has since you brought it to this realm."

"If you don't mind, I'd like to show it to Cassie. One part, in particular."

Kezia sets her cup and saucer on the end table. "Of course I don't mind. Let's go to the study." She rises from her chair with no effort, nearly springing to her feet. She might be seriously ancient, but she's definitely not showing it.

We follow Kezia further into her amazing house, where she leads us into a room lined with bookshelves holding row upon row of books, most of them thick and bound with leather. Like the rest of the house, the ceiling is high enough that there's a library ladder on rollers. The room also features lustrous mahogany walls, a gleaming cherry wood desk and plush leather wing chairs. One of those chairs is occupied, although I'm the only one who seems to notice the woman sitting there.

She appears to have been about fifty when she died. Although, no longer being alive doesn't seem very much on her mind as she relaxes with a book of her own, presumably a spectral version of one of those held within this room. She glances up just briefly, her eyes lingering on Kezia for a moment as a soft smile graces her lips. Then she returns to her reading.

"I remember this room." Cade says, his tone nostalgic. "You've kept building your collection, haven't you?"

Kezia's gaze runs over the shelves of books. "A little. Perhaps not with volumes quite as unique as those you supplied, and definitely not as much since my wife passed away. God rest her soul."

Cade speaks softly. "I heard Josephina had passed. I was so sorry to hear it."

Kezia sighs. "Well, it's been a few years now. You know what they say. You don't get over it, but you do get used to it." She turns to me and brightens her expression. "Of all the rooms in this house, this was Josephina's favorite. She hardly ever stopped reading. In fact, she kindled my love of books to begin with, a very long time ago."

I glance over at the ghost again. Being the topic of conversation appears to have caught her interest, since she's looked up from her reading.

"Oh, well," Kezia says. "I'm sure she's here with me in spirit."

"I'm sure she is," I say.

Kezia looks around again. "Now where is that book? I swear sometimes I'd lose my head if it wasn't attached to my neck."

"I believe it's up there," Cade points to one of the highest shelves.

"Isn't that funny," Kezia says. "Josephina always felt we should keep the more obscure items higher up, while I argued that those books were the ones we'd most often reference. Apparently, she keeps getting her way since, no matter how often I move them down, they somehow find their way up there again."

Josephina looks up again, this time her eyes meeting mine. She nods almost imperceptibly, a slight smile tugging at the corner of her lips.

"I guess those books must just want to live there," I say.

Kezia chuckles. "Well, I guess so." Without another word, she grabs hold of the library ladder, rolls it along the wall and climbs up with the agility of an acrobat. She hops back down to the floor, now holding what I'd guess to be one of the thicker volumes, bound in brown leather and its pages edged with gold leaf. She brings the book to the desk, where we gather around it.

Kezia looks at Cade. "Now, which part did you want to share with your friend?"

"In one of your lectures, you talked about the section on Sativola."

Kezia's gaze drifts to me again, her expression returning to that inquisitive look she displayed when asking when I'd first started visiting Silvermist. "That's certainly an interesting passage," she says. "Perhaps one of the most interesting in the book."

Kezia gently opens the volume, her fingers quickly finding their way to pages nearly at the back. I gasp inwardly at the richly colorful illustration that page holds. Depicted there is a striking woman wearing a flowing black dress and a gray fur robe. She has long red hair, high cheekbones and dark eyes that seem somehow luminous even in the pages of a book. I recognize her instantly as the woman I envisioned when I discovered the alcove in Luchtane Ferndelm's study. It's the same woman I instinctively thought of as a queen of the witches. I can still hear her voice within my mind, from that moment when she guided me to safety. *Use your magic while you can.*

That page, and the one across from it, are also lined with an ornately rendered, flowing script that at first glance reminds me of calligraphy seen through Julia's eyes, back when she took an interest in dead languages. Sanskrit is the one that comes to mind. As I stare, the letters blur and then transform, becoming crisp again before my eyes.

"These pages are written in ancient fae, a language called Eredine. I'm afraid you won't be able to read it, but I'm more than happy to—"

"I can read it." My words come out before I think to stop myself, even as an icy sense of foreboding rises inside me at making the truth known.

But it's already too late and I've spilled my secret. Kezia and Cade share an intense, silent exchange, their expressions revealing shock at what I just said. But my attention immediately returns to those pages, as my eyes travel down the text written there: *Of Unseelie Prince Galen and Human Witch Sativola, Chronicled by Breslor, Born of the Human Realm and Scribe for Emiron, Leader of the Human Tribe Called Milesians, as Transcribed by Kordec of the Seelie Winter Court Following the Battles of Tailtiu and Meath.*

Yeah, it's a mouthful of a title, but immediately I have to wonder. What could a human have written that the fae felt important enough to steal and translate for future generations to be preserved within a monastery archive? I keep reading, the rest of the world forgotten, as within me that sense of foreboding continues to grow.

CHAPTER 4

The pages tell the story of a human woman named Sativola, who was considered to be the most powerful witch of her time. It was said among humans that she could open the veil between this world and the next, that she could prevent unwanted intrusions into the human realm, and that she could step out of her body and walk with the dead.

When the fae first took their place alongside mankind, they were welcomed as benevolent beings of light, noble gods who could perform amazing feats of magic. To the humans, they were known as the Tuatha Dé Danann, meaning "tribe of the gods." In the human realm, these beings were immortal, further confirming the belief that they were deities.

Sativola fell in love with one of these gods. Galen, the High Prince of the Summer Court, who was in turn taken with her exotic beauty and power. Those of the Summer Court had been the first of the Tuatha Dé Danann to evolve toward a state allowing them access to scintillia, the elemental forces that the humans called magic, and it was believed by the humans that those forces had been bestowed upon them because they were noble and good.

Galen had been the sole heir to the crown, and was next in line to become the leader of his people as High King. Afraid of his growing magical power, as well as his influence and esteem amongst the humans, the Winter Court launched a plot to murder both Galen and his father, bringing an end to the line of those upon whom the forces of magic had been originally bestowed. The Winter Court nobles cast the blame for those crimes on the Summer Court, declaring them the Unseelie, those not worthy of holding magic.

Unsure herself who to blame, Sativola turned against the fae race as a whole. In the wars that followed, as the humans fought to expel the fae from their realm, Sativola played a pivotal role, both advising the human armies who'd joined together from different regions, and uniting her fellow witches in the struggle. It was the witches who brought about the turning point, eventually accomplishing the banishment of the fae, and it was Sativola herself who cast the spell closing the veil to a race of beings no longer welcomed by mankind.

According to the narrative later stolen by the fae, over a year later Sativola found herself to be pregnant. In that time, it was said she hadn't been with a human man. It was within this first half-fae, half-human child that Sativola somehow passed on the magic used to create the spell closing the human realm to the fae, and that this same incantation would be carried forth in all future generations of this same bloodline. One human witch would always carry the key within her.

If what I've read is true, it provides the answer to one of the questions that has been plaguing me since all of this started. What advantage did the fae find in physically inhabiting the human realm? Now, it looks like I finally know.

I look up, my eyes meeting Kezia's. "Is it true, that in our realm they were immortal?"

She nods. "Yes, in that they didn't die of natural causes. For over five-hundred years, not one of them passed away. Humans thought they couldn't be killed at all until the wars proved otherwise. If gravely wounded, and denied the chance to heal themselves with magic, they succumbed. What the humans discovered was that the fae were impervious to disease and aging, but a good old iron sword could put an end to them."

Well, there it is. It looks like Cade's theory about the fae and iron really does have a basis in history. But it's the veil witch angle which piques my interest most. In particular, that the human realm once again proved to be a very valuable piece of real estate for interdimensional intruders. That same treasure of immortality is what also drew the Vamanec P'yrin, although in their case immortality was achieved through continually inhabiting one human body after another.

In many ways that's similar to what the fae achieve through their changelings, but there must be some aspect for them that's not the same. Could it be a matter of distance, that changeling magic provides only a muted sort of access? That has to be it, that they can be both in the human realm and not at the same time, the experience somehow filtered. Like remote viewing, but using what amounts to a flesh and blood robot.

As for the rest of what I read, it leaves only more questions. Sativola was a veil witch, obviously, and the idea of her being the most powerful witch of her time I find both exciting and a little frightening. As I have so many times, I think about how Autumn and I were first met with fear and suspicion by our fellow witches. We came to learn that veil witches had been thought to no longer exist, but also had a history of possessing a kind of magic both different and more powerful than that of other witches.

And what of the part about Sativola being able to leave her body and walk the realm of the dead? But it's not even that aspect causing the chill within me to keep spreading. Instead, it's what was at the end of the passage I just read.

I look back and forth between Kezia and Cade again. "Is it possible that she could somehow pass down this magic within her bloodline?"

They regard me solemnly for a moment before Kezia speaks.

"The idea made me curious too," she says. "Enough so that I've researched the idea. First, though, may I ask you a question, Cassie?"

I feel pretty sure what that question is, but I keep my eyes on hers. "Of course."

"Are you a witch?"

I hesitate, and then nod. "Yes. Why did you think so?"

"Well, it's what you said before. You only recently started coming here. Typically, those of us with fae blood find our way here much sooner, but something kept you from doing so."

"Oh, I'm not—" I stop mid-sentence, as the chill keeps spreading. Could it be possible? Suddenly, I think of how little I really know about myself. I only recently learned that my great grandmother had been locked away in an asylum for claiming to see supernatural beings, and that despite attempting suicide on several occasions, she was unable to die until old age took her many years later. Neither my sister nor I even knew we were witches until this year. Who can say how much more we don't know?

As if suspecting the connection I just made, Kezia waits for me to look at her again. When I do, she says, "There are two reasons why this world calls out to us. One of them is because part of us belongs here. This is the world of the half-fae, after all. The other reason is to possess that which we don't in the human realm, that other part of our birthright."

"Magic," I say.

Kezia nods. "Exactly. To possess magic. However, as a witch you weren't denied magic, were you?"

I hesitate again for just a moment, but then say, "No, I wasn't."

I may not have known I was a witch, but magic found me all the same, appearing first in the form of glowing orbs floating toward my outstretched hands when I was five years old.

"And you also found your way to the magical community that most strongly called out to you? That of your fellow witches?"

"Yes," I say, because essentially it's true. My journey was circuitous, to say the least, my path blocked by forces beyond my control. Still, I arrived within that community all the same.

"Thank you for satisfying my curiosity," Kezia says. "After all, I couldn't help wonder why Cade wanted to share this particular aspect of human and fae history."

Unfortunately, his reason for doing so seems perfectly clear. He suspects a connection. Given what I've experienced, I can't help but suspect one too. And the idea terrifies me.

Kezia closes the book, trailing her slender fingers along the length of its cover. "To answer your question from before, my research taught me a few things about how magic differs between that of witches, that of half-bloods and the fae. For example, like witches, the full-blood fae can cast certain kinds of spells. The magic we possess in this realm as half-bloods may be wondrous in many ways, but it's limited. One of those limitations is that we can't cast spells upon each other. In the human realm, of course, we possess no magic at all other than the ability to cast simple glamours. But there's another aspect to casting spells I never knew of before. Not until that particular passage piqued my curiosity." Kezia softly taps the book for emphasis. "And that involves what's called a living spell. Whether this applies to the fae or not, I can't say. However, I've read that certain human witches, those with sufficient power, can keep a spell in place even after leaving their realm."

"You mean after they died," Cade says.

"Exactly. As indicated here." She taps the book again. "And a living spell can't be achieved using an object. While a charmed object can help safeguard a spell—give it a fighting chance, if you will—the only way to keep a spell truly alive is by passing along the incantation used in creating it to someone still living."

I speak softly. "Even if they remain unaware."

"Apparently," Kezia says, lifting the book from the desk.

"Tell her about the other part," Cade says. When Kezia cocks her head in curiosity, he adds, "When you lectured, you mentioned something about the Seelie hold on power."

Kezia shifts her attention back to me. "Well, it's believed by some that those of Galen's line were the true heirs to magic in the faerie realm, and that it was only by ending their line that the Winter Court was able to seize control. It's also believed that it will be one of Sativola's descendants who will bring about the downfall of the Seelie. You can imagine why so many wish to see that happen. For the Unseelie, that would mean an end to oppression. For our kind, it would mean there's no longer anything stopping us from coming and going from Faerie. Perhaps living there, if we so choose."

Suddenly, I realize why Cade has shown such a keen interest in me, and why he's taken such seemingly unnecessary risks. That moment of when we first crossed over into Faerie comes back to me, when that man Brevlane asked if he should tell Dabria that he and Cade had encountered each other. I remember Cade's defeated response when he told Brevlane that it might be better if Dabria didn't know. What I heard in his voice at that moment was pure sadness and futility. What had Cade said when I asked if the Seelie had taken someone from him? *They keep someone from me.*

As Kezia crosses the room to put the book away, another thing occurs to me and I give words to the thought. "But if it's true that one of Sativola's descendants somehow holds the key keeping her spell alive, couldn't that same key be used to break the spell?"

Kezia turns when she gets to the ladder. And this time, when the ghost across the room looks up, she keeps her eyes on me instead of her still living wife.

"I suppose that's entirely possible," Kezia says. "So, I would imagine that this person—whoever he or she turns out to be—would be well advised to stay away from Faerie. I can't imagine anything the fae might want more than to discover who it is."

CHAPTER 5

We trek back across town as a million thoughts swirl through my mind. There's no doubt that Cade was right about that book in Kezia's library being a real eye opener. If even half of that stuff is true, it still explains a lot. Such as why the Seelie are seeking a certain kind of magic using changelings. Namely, the kind of magic that could potentially open the veil between the fae and human realm.

Is that the kind of magic I displayed in being able to visit Faerie? I'm far from convinced that's the case. As far as I know, other witches might be able to do the same. In fact, it might even be possible that all veil witches can, and that ability has nothing to do with keeping the interdimensional door locked. On the other hand, if Autumn has been experiencing anything like that she definitely would have told me. I'm not proud of it, but of the two of us I'm the one usually keeping secrets. Most of the time, that's done to protect my sister, but they're secrets all the same.

Okay, so it's probably safe to assume that, of the two of us, I'm the only one who's been accidentally popping up in Faerie. It also seems suspicious that my visits to that other realm coincided with a seemingly increased presence of changelings within my own. All the same, that still could be nothing but a coincidence, something catching our attention that wouldn't have before. Presumably, changelings have been poking their noses into human affairs for hundreds of years and we just didn't know. And by 'we' I mean humans, since obviously the half-bloods have known all along. So, there's another secret I'm now holding, although it's not one I intend to keep.

"Doing okay?" Cade looks over at me, and I realize I've barely said a word since leaving Kezia's house.

"You know, it really could just be coincidental," I say. "I mean, there's weird stuff going on all over the place. Maybe it's just the magical imbalance that allowed me to cross into Faerie to begin with." I'm not sure even I believe that, but I sure as shit don't want to believe I'm carrying some sort of magical implant. Not to mention carrying the load of being Cade's only hope.

"I don't know," Cade says. "I mean, I guess."

Right, he's not buying it either. This sucks. Like I haven't been kicked around enough by magic in my life. Starting with being sniffed out by the Vamanec P'yrin as a little girl when they sensed my presence.

Oh.

Remembering that definitely doesn't help, since it only serves to underscore something else I was wondering about. If Autumn and I are possibly both descendants of some super powerful veil witch who had a thing for banging faeries, wouldn't Autumn be just as likely to carry the same magical code, message, key, or whatever the heck it is? I mean, genetically we're nearly identical. Hell, we even look like twins.

But there's always been a difference between us, hasn't there? I've always been more magically powerful, and magic has consistently found me first, starting with when we were just kids. In fact, I've always functioned like some sort of magical beacon, making my presence known to other supernatural entities without even trying.

We get back to Cade's apartment, he lets us in, and I rear back in terror as a giant, furry black form flies across the room roaring and baring its teeth. Damn, Hellhound freaks me out every time. Thankfully, Cade is the target for his affection, displayed like most predators going for the kill. He knocks Cade to the ground and stands on his chest growling and whipping his stubby tail back and forth.

"Get off me, you big idiot!" Cade laughs and struggles his way out from beneath his dog, waving his hand through the air to make the lights come on.

Meanwhile, Hellhound advances on me. "Hi boy," I say, backing up a step. "Good boy."

Hellhound leaps, knocks me over and pins me to the floor, this time slapping my face repeatedly with his giant tongue. Finally, Cade drags him off.

"Sorry, he gets excited if I've been away," Cade explains, himself now being head-butted against his stomach until he backs into a wall. Cade vigorously massages Hellhound's massive head until the combination of dog and grizzly bear starts to calm down. Cade then heads toward the kitchen. "Come on, boy. Let's get you something to eat." Hellhound follows at his heels and a moment later Cade calls out an admonishing, *"Hellhound!"*

Presumably, Hellhound has knocked over the table again, but for all I know he may have eaten the refrigerator.

I climb to my feet, pulling my t-shirt up to dry my face. Gross. Thankfully, this time I at least prepared by packing a quick bag so I can change later. Although, I'm beginning to wonder if I should start leaving a few things at Cade's place. Okay, that's a weird thought.

Cade emerges again and says, "Glad to see Isaac and Sloane have been letting Hellhound in. Although, it might work out better if they let him into *their* apartment."

"Well, he is your, um, dog."

"I like to think of Hellhound as everyone's dog."

Hellhound continues to pant and stare up at him, suggesting he might have a different opinion on the subject.

"By the way, are Sloane and Isaac a couple?" I guess it doesn't really matter, but I'm just curious.

"God no," Cade says. "That would be disastrous to a partnership like ours. It's stressful enough wondering who's going to make it back alive, without that someone being your significant other."

Which begs the question, "Have you ever considered possibly not stealing from the fae?"

"Seelie fae," Cade corrects me. "And with any luck I can retire soon."

I decide not to pursue that cryptic response, since I think I know where he's going. I'm not up for having that particular conversation. I only stopped inwardly freaking out a few minutes ago.

"Come on, let's go upstairs," Cade says. "I hope you brought Sloane's amulet."

*

As we climb the stairs, you can hear Isaac's and Sloane's raised voices out in the hall. If I was to guess, I'd say they're continuing the same argument we heard at the gathering of Silvermist occupants earlier tonight.

"I just think we need to do something!" Sloane says, her voice raised in pitch as well as volume.

Isaac counters with, "And I think there's way more at stake here!" What he feels to be at stake, we don't learn in that moment since Cade says, "See what I mean? Definitely not a couple."

At least not a happy one, I think, as Cade knocks on the door.

Their voices cut off and a moment later Isaac calls out, "Who goes there, friend or fae?"

I can't help but crack a smile, even though Cade says, "It really does get old after a while."

We enter the apartment to find Isaac where we found him last time, sitting on the sofa polishing his guitar. Sloane stands at the window with her back to us, her raised shoulders signaling that she's still tense from the conversation we just interrupted. Beyond her, a spark of light streaks through the sky.

"Everything okay, guys?" Cade says.

"So, you're alive." Isaac's casual tone suggests that it's not that unusual for one of them to disappear for a week. Or maybe, given what they do, downplaying their worry is just part of the game. Like Cade just said, they can never be sure that one of them will make it back again.

"Still kicking," Cade says. "Remember Cassie?"

It's really just his way of letting Sloane know he didn't come alone. She turns from the window and her expression softens as her anger fades. She offers me a smile.

"Hi, Cassie. Nice to see you again." She turns to Cade. "Sure, everything's okay. But Isaac here thinks we should just ignore the situation in Faerie and go on with business as usual."

Isaac shakes his head and sets his guitar down with a thunk against the rug. He speaks softly, not looking at any of us. "That's not what I said."

Sloane narrows her eyes. "That's what I heard."

I get one of those strange tingling feelings on the back of my neck, the very sensation Julia has told me to watch for. A sudden itch on the lobe of one ear, or the side of your nose. A strange spasm at the side of your eye. Most people think these are just random physical occurrences. Meaningless inconveniences to be ignored. Psychics know otherwise. Those are signals, the more deeply attuned part of yourself trying to gain your attention. Julia even swears that the different locations on your skin carry different meanings. The problem being, this time I'm not sure what just gave me a psychic ping.

"What was your take on the situation?" I ask Isaac.

His eyes meet mine, and then he looks toward Cade. Again, he speaks quietly, when what we heard climbing the stairs was a much more forceful exchange. "I just think we have bigger fish to fry."

Cade, having become the recipient of that vague response, shakes his head. "What do you mean?"

Isaac picks up his guitar again and cradles it in his lap. "Obviously, we can't ignore the situation in Faerie. I wish we could. I just think there are much larger stakes at play here."

I get another tingle on the back of my neck. "As in?"

This time, I see an unexpected anger in Isaac's gaze. "As in the human realm. The place where we were born. That's what we should be worried about, not Faerie."

Sloane leaves her post at the window and walks toward us, her attention focused on Isaac. "None of this is affecting that realm. It's only here that shit is going on, and in Faerie from what we hear."

Isaac mutters, "Right, but isn't it only a matter of time?"

Again, he looks at everyone but me, and now I think I know why I just got those psychic signals. Maybe it's something Cade told Isaac before I met them, or something Isaac and Sloane discussed after I did. I just don't know. But the feeling I get is that Isaac is worried about the same aspect I brought up back at Kezia's house. What if all of this has been about the Seelie searching for the magic keeping them locked out of the human realm? Is it possible that they've been searching for hundreds of years? The answer to that, I believe, is yes. That they started searching as soon as Sativola closed off the realm to them, and that they haven't stopped since.

"That might be a stretch, but whatever," Sloane says, clearly trying to break the tension. She turns to Cade. "So, how did it go? I'm assuming you must have struck out."

Cade stares back at her, a mildly smug expression on his face.

Sloane's eyes widen, and then her jaw drops as she draws in a sudden breath. "No freaking way." Her eyes pivot to me. "You actually did it?"

My face grows warm. Still, I can't help but feel a little proud. "One of them."

It's strange to realize that, going in, I thought first and foremost about rescuing Julia. And, if possible, liberating Ellie. But my list has grown since then to include Helen, Lily and Mitch. How many more are held there, though, and for what reasons?

"A changeling," Cade says.

Sloane does an excited little dance. "Are you kidding me? No way! Seriously?"

"Yeah, seriously," Cade says.

I can't help but notice that Isaac doesn't seem nearly as excited. He's smiling, but his expression seems a bit forced.

Cade notices too. "Don't you think that's amazing?"

Isaac nods. "It really is. Congratulations. Hey, why don't I go get us something to drink? I think we still have some wine. How does that sound?"

Cade cocks his head. "Sure, that sounds great. Thanks, Isaac."

Isaac goes into the kitchen and Cade speaks softly to Sloane, "What's up with him?"

She shakes her head, and speaks just above a whisper. "Not sure. I guess all of this just has him freaked out."

As soon as she says it, the building around us trembles. I sway on my feet and clutch Cade's arm to keep from stumbling.

"Earthquakes are part of it," he says. "Revlen says it's been bad on their side."

"What a mess," Sloane says. "But I guess it stands to reason. I mean, something is bound to go haywire if you keep trying to hog all of the magic."

"Oh, right." Cade digs in his pocket and produces the amulet I gave him as we came upstairs. It just would have been weird if I returned it to her, when she was hesitant loaning it to Cade in the first place. He grins at Sloane and hands it over. "Speaking of hogged magic."

Sloane laughs and displays a mock-indignant expression. "That wasn't hogged magic. That was *saved* magic. There's a difference." She gives the pendant a shake, and then holds it up to the light. "About six months' worth. Half of which appears to be gone now."

I wince. "Sorry about that."

"Don't be," Sloane says. "That's just my way of reminding Cade he owes me."

Cade grins. "Now that I gave it back, do you mind if we borrow that again?"

"Seriously, you're going back already?"

Cade shrugs. "We pretty much have to."

He holds his hand out, and Sloane hesitates. Then she hands the amulet back with a sigh. "Sure. Whatever. At least it went to a good cause last time."

Cade drops onto the sofa. "A very good cause. After all, we've now proved that a changeling spell can be undone. Well, at least we've proved that *Cassie* can undo a changeling spell."

Sloane and I both sit as well. Sloane shakes her head, as if still in disbelief. "And what about in our realm?" Seeing our blank expressions, she adds, "I mean our other realm. Are the number of changelings still increasing there?"

"I wouldn't doubt it," Cade says. "The Seelie have definitely been ramping up their agenda."

It's a good question, and something I've been wondering about too. I didn't see anything in the news last week, but that doesn't really mean anything. Presumably, most people don't report someone they know starting to act different. I've also wondered more than once if the man who tried to kill me might have been a changeling. What other explanation can there be? But if it was a changeling, who was controlling it? And if I carry the magic within me both to keep the veil locked, or to open it again, what would it mean if I died? My guess is it depends on how the spell was cast, but it's always easier to open the door when you have the key.

"And what was with the psychic thing?" Isaac says, returning from the kitchen with a bottle of wine and four glasses. "Did anyone figure out that connection?"

He takes the remaining chair and starts filling the wine glasses. He seems fine now, so maybe he just needed a moment to get past his argument with Sloane. To be fair, we didn't exactly arrive at the best moment.

"I have a theory on that one," I say. "Well, maybe more of a question, but what if they're setting up some sort of network?"

Isaac maintains eye contact this time, that guarded defensiveness from before seeming gone now too. "A network…"

"Right. Maybe they're not just looking for something. Or someone. But they're using psychics to create some sort of connection."

Sloane gasps. "Oh, my God. That makes sense! It's long been suspected that the Seelie have some sort of magical connection going on. No one understands how it works, but it's like first they somehow locked most of the magic down, and then found a way to keep it channeled between them."

"So, you're thinking they're using those psychic kids more like objects than people," Cade says. "Is that it?"

"Wow, imagine that," Sloane says. "The Seelie using someone like an object."

I think of the night Fashenan led me to discover that secret alcove in Luchtane's study, and that luminous globe that rose spinning into the air. It's an important part of this whole thing, I'm sure. Possibly crucial to determining just how the Seelie are controlling the power of the ley line. My heart starts beating fast, and I'm just about to tell them what happened, but then my eyes go to Isaac again as he waits to learn more. Maybe I'm just being paranoid, but I can't forget that psychic ping from before. Especially since I get another one now.

"Like I said, it's just a theory," I say. "Who the hell knows what they're up to?"

CHAPTER 6

The idea is to cross over into Faerie while it's late at night, hoping that we'll find things to be quiet with the city kingdom mostly asleep. Peaceful isn't exactly what we encounter. Instead we find ourselves immersed in chaos.

We no sooner emerge into the Unseelie neighborhood than a platoon of Seelie soldiers charge by on horseback, encircling a crowd that's taken to the street. I shield my eyes against the light of an inferno as a nearby building burns. Acrid smoke stings my nostrils. Suddenly, there's another flare as the man leading the charge unleashes an explosion at the crowd's feet with a thrust of his arm. He has bone white skin, platinum hair tied back flat to his skull and a jagged scar running down his face. Vintain.

The horses come to a stop, rearing up as a group, and then settling to the ground again. The soldiers draw their swords. The crowd is trapped within this bottleneck section of the street and we're penned in with them.

"Quick," Cade says. "Get back to the tunnel!"

But it's already too late. The crowd has filled in behind us, a wall of bodies blocking our way. Firelight flickers across the faces of men and women, their eyes wide in both fury and fear. Some try to fall back, hoping not to be seen, while others yell out angry curses at the Seelie incursion.

Above us, fireballs streak through the sky as they plummet down in the distance.

I'm jostled against Cade as the crowd continues closing in around us. Beside me, a man speaks to the woman with him, his voice a growl of derision. "They're scared is what they are." He points to the sky as another fireball falls. "See that? That's their magic burning."

"And ours along with it," the woman says.

Suddenly, a blast of light shoots toward the sky. It's Vintain again, the torch emanating from his hand, and this time projecting an image into the night. I gasp at what I see above the crowd. It's my face, behind me the misty forms of the Blue Ridge Mountains. Somehow, Vintain captured my image when I went there with him as Grayson.

Vintain's voice roars out to the crowd. "Take a good look at that face! I want you to memorize it!"

The crowd grows quiet and stops shifting. Everyone looks up.

"Has anyone here seen this woman?"

Cade grabs onto my shoulders and spins me around. He keeps one hand on the amulet while waving the other in front of my face. My cheeks start to tingle, and then burn as the heat of magic spreads.

Vintain's voice rings out again. "As I'm sure you can see, that woman is not of this realm."

A woman behind us says, "Must be a half-blood. Look how small her points are."

I can't help but glance up, thinking she must be wrong. I stifle another gasp. Within the projected image, my ears do show slight points. Is it something I've never noticed before, or something that's just recently changed about me? Involuntarily, I reach up to touch my ears and I could swear they feel different.

"She is not of this realm, and yet she has been here," Vintain calls out. "She may be here still. So, I ask again. Has anyone seen this woman? Because if one of you has been harboring her—"

"Death to the Seelie!" The man's voice rings out behind me, a cry of desperate rage. I'm jostled again as he shoves his way forward to hurl a flaming bottle into the air.

The moment hangs frozen, the crowd staring as this gesture of defiance traces a burning arc through the darkness. The bottle lands, and an explosion blooms in a blinding flash of white and orange, flame spreading as fire licks up whatever that bottle held.

Then all hell breaks loose. The Seelie charge forward, Vintain thrusting out his hand to launch a lightning strike of magic. The man falls. People scream in fear as they try to run. It's pandemonium, the crowd pinned with no way to disperse. Those at the back may escape through alleys or adjoining streets, but those of us toward the front are held within the roiling terrified mass.

I'm jostled again, then shoved and pushed. I'm caught by a wave as the crowd splits before the Seelie charge. As if in a nightmare, I see Cade's face on the other side of that gulf. He reaches out to me, his mouth stretched as he calls out. I reach for him too, but it's pointless. We've both been swept up in the stampede. Within seconds, he's swallowed up and gone. It's all I can do to remain on my feet as the crowd keeps pushing against me, taking me with it. Fighting back against the flow would mean getting trampled.

Behind me, another explosion booms against the night. I run with the crowd, turning back to see another building go up in flames. From within it voices cry out and people scream. No one is trying to fight back now or make their anger known. It's down to escape or die trying. I keep working my way toward the outside of the crowd, sliding through gaps whenever I get the chance. Those chances are few and far between, and I don't know how many blocks I'm pushed along with the panicked flow before I manage to get free.

I stand gasping and coughing before an empty storefront. A cloud of dust raised by the stampede swirls through the air. The pane of glass before me suddenly flickers with the light of another falling fireball, and I look up to see my own reflection. An old woman stares back, and I spin around to face her directly. Which makes no sense, I realize, since I saw just one reflection. Of course. Cade's magic. Even now my face tingles. Only in this moment do I realize what he was doing. Casting a glamour, the magic of the fae and half-fae. I turn back to stare at the wizened, gray-haired version of myself that's already starting to fade. I don't know if it's because Cade's now too far away, or if it's due to the Seelie magical stranglehold, but the magic isn't holding. Apparently, I made it this far disguised, but now I watch my own young face emerge from beneath the mask of age.

Behind me, people keep running as the Seelie soldiers advance, leaving a trail of bodies in their wake. I look around for Cade, but see instead two women looking back at me. One of them is young, the other middle-aged. They look like mother and daughter. The younger one points and she cries, "There! I see her!" The older woman cuffs the back of her head, presumably for attempting to help the Seelie. But it's already too late. Heads turn in my direction, and I take off running again, hoping none of the soldiers heard that girl call out.

I'm breathing hard, sweat running down my face, as I keep trying to jostle my way forward. Behind me, another explosion sounds and people stop. They turn back to look, which gives me the break I've been hoping for. I slip through to where the crowd grows more sparse. I see the end of the block now, which means I can at least get off this street. But who can say how many people I'll yet encounter, and if any of them will recognize me?

Shit, Cade, where are you?

But it's not Cade who returns my silent call for help. It's Julia.

Cassie? Are you here? Be careful!

It's that strange connection between us again, Julia somehow knowing I'm in peril. She's never been wrong, not once, even if I've denied it.

I project my thoughts to her, hoping that somehow my message gets through. *I'm coming for you. I'm going to get you out of here.*

I wait to hear her again, but like last time her voice within me falls silent. Again, I think it must have something to do with the gaps in the Seelie stranglehold. Most of the time she's blocked, her psychic abilities muted, but every so often a signal gets through.

The crowd starts moving again and I don't want to lose the advantage I've gained. I've managed getting to the outer rim and sure as hell don't want to become part of the stampede again. All it will take for that to happen is one more act of resistance, or a sudden surge by the Seelie soldiers.

I dash toward the street corner while I still can, having no idea where I'll find myself. My heart pounds in my ears, my breaths coming in short gasps. Questions flood my mind. Why are the Seelie doing this? Do they really think I hold within me that thing they seek? Can't they see the destruction they're doing to themselves? But I know the answer to that, don't I? Of course they do, and that man was right. They *are* scared. They're losing their grip on magical power in this realm, and they're running out of time. But another realm awaits them, one within which they were gods. All they need is the key to get back there again.

The crowd is thinner on the next street. It's also dark, with no light coming from the nearby buildings. Around me, I see shadowy figures, people walking fast and some still running. I hear a man say, "It's only a matter of time now. I can feel it."

As if to emphasize his point, another fireball streaks down above. Then the ground starts to tremble, the vibration continuing to grow until it feels like the entire world is shaking. In the distance, I hear Vintain call out, "Which of you has seen her! The one who tells us the truth will be rewarded!" But even his voice is just one more element of the nightmare surrounding me. I lurch forward, trying to keep from falling or grabbing onto someone. The tremors intensify until it's impossible to keep moving forward. People stagger, some pitching over sideways. I take that moment to drop to one knee, peering around as I try to spot Cade. Still, I don't see him. Is he okay? Did he go looking for me in some other direction? Or is he further down the road, waiting for me to catch up? There's just no way to know, and nothing to be done until the earthquake stops.

It might just be minutes, but it feels like hours as the ground continues to shake. I hear shouts in the distance and what sound like shots. Another explosion rocks the ground, a blast of light flaring up toward the sky where my own image has finally disappeared. Could the Unseelie have started defending themselves? If so, with what? I remember Cade telling me that the Seelie swords were mostly for show, a vestige from when wars were fought that way. Now they fight using magic, as they have for hundreds of years. So, is what I'm hearing the sound of magic coming back to the Unseelie during yet another magical brownout?

I want it to be true, but the weak trickle of magic coursing through me suggests it's not likely. What I'm hearing is probably just more Seelie intimidation.

Finally, the earthquake stops and I get to my feet. Others around me do the same, those who decided it was safer to stay put than to keep trying to run. I trudge alongside others, feeling numb, my ears still ringing and my heart pounding. Fighting continues in the distance, sounding like it moved onto another block as the Seelie keep searching. Something tells me it's going to be a long night for them. The feeling I get is that the ley line hasn't yet been reined into place. It too keeps fighting back, and I can't forget what I felt before when I discovered the alcove. The magic of this world is alive, conscious, and she's looking for a way out. Why now after so long, I don't know, but I feel sure that what my gut tells me is true. A door has opened and the Seelie can't seem to quite close it again.

I'm forced to stop as my path is blocked. I try to make my way around those dark forms. Then another fireball lights up the sky and I see their faces. I've seen these men before, in an alley behind the Gilded Gargoyle.

"Well, hello again," one of them growls. "It would seem you're much more valuable than we thought."

I reach down and unsheathe my athame. I thrust the blade out, pointed directly at his throat. "Come one step closer," I say. "Seriously, do it."

But his words were an attempted distraction to keep me from noticing the one who's crept in beside me. He tries to grab me, and I lash out. He reels back, cursing as blood drips down his face from where I just slashed him. "You're going to pay for that ten times over, bitch," he says.

I back up but I'm surrounded. I keep spinning around and thrusting my blade out. There are four of them, like last time. Their eyes gleam, as do their grins. This is a game to them, one they enjoy. If I had my magic, I could send them flying across the asphalt. If they were vampires in my realm, I could turn them to ash. But I'm not in my realm. Nor do I have the magic I've felt coursing through me here before. A power unlike anything I've known.

Come on, come on, come on! I grit my teeth and reach into my core, willing that power to find me. It doesn't come, even though I could swear I feel it trying.

One of them comes at me again, this time with a blade of his own. I cry out as he slashes my forearm, my own blood spraying against my face. I spin around again, parrying, my pain and fear met with laughter.

"Oh, sweetheart," the leader says. "Do you really think that toy knife is going to stop us?"

"Yeah? Fuck you!" There's no doubt that I'm going down, so I'm taking this asshole with me. That's my entire plan as I charge to plunge my dagger into his stomach. He blocks me, but not before my blade pierces his flesh. He bellows in both rage and pain, having expected me to fold.

I raise my knife to thrust again, when a hand locks onto my wrist, bending it back. Pain sears through me and my hand springs open. My athame drops. From what feels like a mile away, I hear the steely chime of my blade hitting asphalt. This is it. I'm going to end in a very bad way.

Then the one holding me screams out in pain as, behind him, a shadowy figure swoops in. He staggers back, eyes wide and mouth gaping as a blade pierces his chest. He drops to his knees as the blade is withdrawn. Then another man drops, this one slashed across the neck. In mere seconds two men are down.

Now it's just me and the stranger against the two who are left. I snatch up my knife, and then the stranger presses his back to mine. "Steady," he says. "Follow my lead."

My eyes widen at the sound of his voice. How is it possible that he's once again come to my aid? But there's no time to ask as Esras and I now circle together, facing off against the attackers.

The leader closes in again, toward me with his sword drawn. "Maybe they'll pay just for your head," he says.

"Now, spin!" Esras says.

I find myself making my stand against the other. Behind me, I hear the leader's gruff voice. "Gods help me."

"Not likely," Esras says.

We separate as he thrusts out. I hear a scream of pain, and then another. A body hits the ground, and I can't help but grin. The fucker who trapped me before, and tried to again, just met his end. Still, I keep my eyes on my opponent.

He freezes suddenly, looking past me. At seeing Esras, he goes pale. That distraction is all I need. I charge at him blade first, but he's already spinning away, tripping over himself to escape.

Finally, I can turn to face Esras. His eyes stare back into mine, his chest rising and falling. "I'll explain later," he says. "Come on, we need to keep moving."

CHAPTER 7

Esras and I stride through the night, while I scan the dark street seeing only strangers. Many wander dazed, following the violence that just occurred, resulting both from the actions of the Seelie and the protesting environment itself. Even the bodies we just left in our wake are but one more thread in this nightmare tapestry.

"I assume you must be looking for your friend," Esras says. "The half-blood thief you travel with."

My head snaps in his direction, a sense of shock rippling through me. "You know about Cade?"

It's a stupid question. Obviously, he does. But I have no idea how to process the information. Cade is a rebel who steals from the Seelie, wanting nothing more than to see their downfall. Essentially, he's Esras's sworn enemy.

Esras doesn't answer, since there's no reason to. He puts his hand on my arm to guide me past a pile of rubble, debris that must have toppled during the earthquake. With the contact, a rippling warmth flows through me, reminding me of when we rode together upon his horse. The same thing happened that time too. Just being near him sent a pleasant sensation through my body. What the hell is that?

63

"You'll never find him in this melee," Esras says. "And it's much too dangerous to go looking."

He's right, of course. Parting with Esras means death, or possibly something worse. I can't imagine my odds of escaping capture would be good, not when the Seelie know exactly who and what I am. Still, why is Esras helping me again? If anything, he should be furious at my return after he risked so much to help me. I hold my questions for now, as we leave the street and make our way through a series of alleys. They're a study in gloom, filth and age, reminding me that this city must be ancient, hundreds of years older than any human city. Possibly thousands. The conditions surrounding us also remind me that we're not exactly in Scintillia's most upscale neighborhood. Very much the opposite, in fact. For me, that's not a bad thing, but what about Esras?

I turn to him as we weave our way through yet another alley. "Aren't you worried about being seen?"

He cracks a half-grin. "Sure. Aren't you?"

Touché. "Some of us have no other option," I say.

"What makes you think my situation is any different? Look out!"

Esras draws his sword and I look to see a hunched creature blocking our path. It's shaped like a rat, but at least five feet long and covered with spines. Red eyes gleam at us hungrily as it opens its mouth to reveal razor fangs.

I draw my own blade too. "What the hell is that thing?"

"Golork. They're drawn to the smell of blood."

I assume he means fae. "What about human blood?"

Even as I say it, I get a sinking feeling. With everything that's happened, I've managed to ignore the wound I sustained in the struggle. I realize now that the hand I'm using to hold my athame is sticky and slick.

"It would appear they might be even more drawn to human blood," Esras says.

"Great," I say through gritted teeth. Could this night get any more messed up?

The golork advances, hissing as its spines bristle. A fireball streaks down above, its orange glow reflecting off talons I didn't see before.

"Maybe we should use another alley." It seems common sense to me, since there's clearly no shortage. There has to be another way of getting to wherever we're going.

"Once a golork smells blood, it won't back off."

"Awesome."

Esras steps toward the thing, sword held ready. "This one seems particularly aggressive."

"Yeah, I noticed."

The golork rears back, and then leaps toward us. Esras jumps forward, thrusting out his blade to catch the creature mid-air. The thing lets out a piercing scream, five times louder and more shrill than anything I've heard come out of a creature on Earth. The golork thuds to the ground, letting out several more piercing howls, each one corresponding with a thrust of Esras's sword. My ears are literally ringing against the pitch and volume, but at least the damn thing appears to be dead.

"You make that look easy," I say, bending down to strap my athame into its sheath.

"Golorks aren't particularly bright," Esras says. "But they're sure as hell loud."

"Yeah, I noticed that too."

Esras's eyes meet mine. "Which means everyone within ten blocks now knows someone who's bleeding just came through these alleys. Come on, we better keep moving."

At that same moment another sound cuts through the air, this time the wail of a klaxon horn. It keeps growing louder, rising and falling throughout the city. There's no doubt it can be heard for miles.

"What the hell is that about?"

Esras sighs. "They've called a military curfew. Anyone seen out after this will be killed on sight."

CHAPTER 8

We make our way through more alleys, thankfully without encountering any more golorks. We enter one more, which we follow until it ends at a stone wall. Even in the dark, I can see that it's thick with moss and ivy. I assume Esras has his act together better than to get us lost, and I'm proved right when he performs a series of precise hand motions. A seam appears in the stone, etched at first in blue light, and then widening into a gap big enough to step through.

I hesitate, instinct telling me I have no idea what's behind that stone wall or if I'll be able to get out again. I'm being ridiculous, I know. Esras didn't just rig a sword fight and a creepy creature encounter to gain my trust. In fact, he's repeatedly risked his life to help me. Obviously, I can trust him. One of these days maybe I'll face the fact that I've been traumatized in twenty different ways, at least, and find myself a decent therapist. No wonder things didn't work out with Phoenix.

The magical door slides closed behind us, and we descend a stone staircase leading to another door, this one a thick slab of wood. It too swings open upon Esras issuing another fluid gesture. Not for the first time, it occurs to me that he retains his ability to perform magic when my own abilities remain somehow blocked. Of course, there can only be one reason. Because he's Seelie. Which isn't exactly working as a disadvantage at the moment, but it does seem a little ironic. After all, he's currently aiding the very person who, if what Cade hopes is true, could ultimately relieve him of his magical power. Which once again begs the question. Why does Esras keep helping me?

Beyond the door, I half-expect to find a gloomy cellar with spider webs and scuttling rats. Instead, we enter a chamber that looks surprisingly comfortable. The walls are indeed stone, but they're smooth and painted light blue. The floor is mostly covered by a plush, ornately woven rug of green and gray hues. There's also a sofa, a couple of sitting chairs and a table. The wall displays a large map of Scintillia, the Barrens and the country beyond, which isn't someplace I've considered before. I've always assumed everything beyond the city kingdom to be wasteland, but while the map depicts the Barrens in white, the territories farther out are shaded tan and green. As I take in the room, I get the feeling it's a place where people meet. A secret place, obviously, given how we entered.

Now that we finally stopped moving, and seem to be out of danger, everything I've been through hits me like a freight train. My legs feel like lead, my entire body aches, and I'm suddenly dizzy. Enough so, that I feel unsteady on my feet. I feel flushed, and I peel off my jacket to see the gash upon my upper arm. Blood continues to flow from it, collecting on the dried blood originating from when I first suffered the wound. The sight does nothing to lessen my lightheadedness. I drop onto the sofa, being careful to keep my arm above my blood-spattered jeans. They're trash now anyway, so I might as well spare the nice rug.

"Good idea," Esras says. "Take a seat." I'm about to tell him it's not like I had a choice, when he adds, "I'll be right back."

He leaves the room and I let out a sigh. I sink back, resting my head against the sofa as I close my eyes. A hundred images flicker through my mind. I see burning buildings, Seelie soldiers, and the frightened faces of the crowd. I see Cade's desperate expression as he reached out to me through the human tidal wave. I see those men who confronted me, and that moment of death for one of them as Esras's blade pierced his chest. The image that keeps playing over and over again, though, is that of Vintain sitting upon his horse, as he disdainfully beheld the people he'd come to intimidate.

That was the first time I truly saw his face. Before that, I'd seen him only in a dream, one I'll never forget. It happened on the night when I'd been just about to invite Grayson into my bed. Suddenly, a bad feeling had washed over me. I'd made up an excuse and gotten out of the car. Thank God I did. I shudder now to think how close I came to having sex with him.

"Feeling any better?"

My eyes pop open at the sound of Esras's voice, and I see the concern in his eyes. Definitely a welcome sight compared to what I just saw inside my mind. The truth is, he'd be a welcome sight anytime, which isn't something I ever imagined feeling about a man whose ears rise into points. But there's no denying that he's handsome. Stunning, in fact, with his tall and muscular physique, and his perfect face framed in lustrous black hair. There's no doubt that he inherited his mother's physical beauty. Thankfully, he doesn't appear to have inherited much else in the way of her personality traits, if any at all.

Esras carries a basin to the sofa and takes a seat beside me. The basin holds soapy water, as well as a cloth, which Esras wrings out as he keeps his eyes on mine. "May I?" he says.

I nod and roll the sleeve of my t-shirt up onto my shoulder, doing my best not to wince. I really don't want to look, but it's not like I have a choice. The gash is puckered wide, oozing blood and what I'm pretty sure is pus. The skin around it is inflamed and red. Shit. This can't be good. Who the hell knows what kind of bacteria might exist in Faerie that's lethal to humans? Who knows when the scumbag who stabbed me last washed the blade of his dagger? If he ever did. Or how many bodies it had been plunged into before he was brought to an end by a blade himself.

Great. I've kicked the asses of vampires, demons and nasty-ass ghosts. Not to mention body-snatchers. And I'm about to be brought down by a faery infection. Definitely didn't see that one coming. Then again, it's hard to anticipate getting stabbed while visiting a place that's not supposed to exist.

Esras gently presses the cloth to my arm, above the cut, and the soapy water both stings and feels like heaven. I buck in my seat as I draw in a sharp breath.

"Doing okay?" he says.

I look into his eyes and nod. "Yes."

He submerges the cloth and wrings it out again. I glance down to see blood spreading through the basin, pink tendrils floating out beneath the suds.

"It might be better not to look," Esras says. "Maybe try closing your eyes."

"Yeah, good idea." I do as advised and let my head sink back again.

As Esras continues cleaning the wound, that pleasant warmth from before returns and starts to flow through me. As the seconds pass, the sensation keeps growing stronger. He keeps wringing out the cloth and pressing it to my skin, gently rubbing up and down my arm. It makes no sense, but soon that rippling warmth vibrates through my entire body. The good news is that I'm no longer feeling the burning pain of the knife wound. The bad news is that I'm suddenly horny as hell. To the point where, when Esras touches me again, my legs go slack and I let out a soft moan.

"Did I hurt you? I'm sorry."

My eyes pop open and I see that same concerned expression, when I almost expected a knowing smile. He has no idea what his touch does to me? It would appear not, thankfully. Right now, I just don't need to hand over control like that. Not a good idea. Right?

"Should I keep going?"

Oh, shit. I hesitate, and then say, "Yes, please. I mean, you probably should."

"Okay, try to relax. This shouldn't take long."

Take all the time you need. "Okay."

I close my eyes, settle back again, and listen as Esras rinses the cloth. He brings it back to my skin, gently rubbing. And, yes, it happens again. That pleasant warmth vibrates through me, rippling out from my core. If this guy was a doctor in the human realm, women would be lined up around the block. Or guys. Whatever. No judgement. But, oh my God. At least this time I manage to keep my mouth shut and don't let out anymore involuntary gasps of pleasure.

Am I supposed to feel pleasure when a being from another realm cleans a knife wound on my arm? I highly doubt this. Yes, I need to find a therapist as soon as I get back.

"Okay, it looks clean," Esras says. "You should be good."

Really? Damn. I open my eyes as he sets the cloth back into the basin. He puts that on the floor and I dare to look at the gash on my arm. It definitely looks better, but it's still gaping and inflamed.

"That looks pretty good," I say.

I mean, I don't want to sound ungrateful, and it's not like he can whisk me out to some fae emergency room. I guess they must have something like that around here, but there's the military curfew to consider. Plus the fact that I'm a human witch who has just scored the number one spot in the Seelie "Most Wanted" list.

Esras nods and inspects the wound again. "I agree. Cleaning it first seems to make a difference. Now, let's see about healing it."

Huh?

He raises his hands, fingers spread, and closes his eyes. His face remains still, but just a slight tightening at the corner of his eyes tells me that he's concentrating. The warm vibration from before rises again inside me. It spreads through my body, tickling all of my senses. Soon, it's at least three times stronger than before, while continuing to get more intense. I can barely think.

"Oh, God."

"Are you okay?"

"Yes."

"Keep going?"

"I think you should."

"Are you sure?"

"Definitely."

The vibration grows even stronger, and then stronger again. It takes everything I have not to cry out. It literally feels like his magic is mingling with my own, at least the magic that's buried deep within me. Part of me knows this is absolutely ridiculous, that I've lost all control. Most of me doesn't care. *Keep it together, Cassie*, I tell myself. *Just keep it together. This is strictly professional.*

I hang onto the absurdity of the thought that there could be anything normal about what I'm experiencing, and I make it through without succumbing completely. Just barely.

I come to my senses when I hear Esras's voice again. He sounds pleased this time. "Much better. Have a look."

I do, and I gasp at what I see. My arm looks perfectly normal, my skin pink and glowing. The only sign that I was even cut shows on the back of my hand and around my fingers, where brown crusty blotches still show from where blood ran down my arm.

Despite how many times I've seen magic, I can't help but say, "That's amazing."

Esras smiles, and I realize it's the first time I've seen him do so. His expression softens, his eyes light up, and all the tension leaves his face. I see a kind person looking back at me, and I feel like a complete fool for having doubted him.

I hear a voice inside me say, *Therapy, girl. Therapy.*

"Would you like to take a shower?" Esras says.

My eyes rivet back to his again. I open my mouth but no words come out.

Esras nods toward the door. "It's just down the hall. I also left some clothes in there for you. I'm not sure if they'll fit, but at least they're clean."

Right, okay. He means shower alone. Not my first choice, but probably a good idea. As for clothes, who cares if they fit? Mine stink of smoke and they're covered with blood. Amazingly, Esras looks to have come through fairly unscathed. Okay, whatever. He's good with a sword. Put him up against a vampire and let's see what happens.

CHAPTER 9

It would appear that the time I spent resting, along with Esras working his fae mojo on me, has put enough strength back into my legs that I make it out the door and down the hall. I see only one lit doorway, which proves to be a bathroom. And, as Esras said, there is indeed a shower, along with a folded towel and a bundle of clothes. Where they came from, I really don't care. I turn on the water, strip down and get in as soon as steam starts to rise.

By the time I get back, Esras has removed all traces of putting me back together. The basin is gone, and I don't want to know where. The sooner I forget getting slashed open, the better. He stands regarding the map on the wall, but turns as I come into the room.

"Oh, good, they fit," he says.

By which he means the clothes I now wear, dark brown leather pants and a light green blouse, embroidered at the collar and with long billowing sleeves. I've rolled the sleeves up because they're annoying.

"Who do they belong to?"

Esras shakes his head, as if I just said something that makes no sense. "You," he says.

Oh. Right. He just gave them to me. Different culture. Presumably here, who the clothes belonged to before no longer matters. A gift is a gift.

"Thank you."

"You're welcome. How's your arm?"

"Perfect," I say, because it's true. I hold it out for him to see. My arm looks like nothing ever happened.

Esras nods, apparently satisfied. "Well, it helped that the wound was still fresh. I doubt we would have seen the same kind of result if much more time had passed. In that case, you'd almost certainly have a scar."

Talk about humble. The guy just made an infected dagger wound disappear and he's acting like he did an acceptable job washing the dishes. But the conversation offers an opening into that other thing I was wondering about before. Although I try to approach it diplomatically.

"If you could still use magic, why didn't you use it against those guys?" I mean, it only makes sense. Why go at it with swords when you can take care of things with a few hand gestures and possibly an incantation?

Esras hesitates as he considers. I can also tell from his expression that the subtext didn't escape his notice. *If you could still use magic. As in you, not me.* Then he shrugs and says, "My viewpoint on the use of magic differs from that shared by many of my people. As you've probably observed, our methods aren't sustainable."

I plop down onto the sofa again, letting out a satisfied sigh. Ladylike as always. Esras opts for one of the chairs. Damn.

"Yeah, I've noticed. What's your viewpoint?"

Again, Esras hesitates, and the feeling I get is that his opinion isn't one he often shares openly. "Personally, I don't believe magic should be used for confrontational purposes. Not unless the circumstances are particularly dire."

"You don't consider four guys with daggers a dire circumstance?"

The corner of Esras's mouth quirks as he resists a smile. I can tell he's trying not to seem egotistical. Definitely humble.

"Well, they didn't strike me as being particularly skilled," he says. "Their kind never are. They spend their lives intimidating the vulnerable and outnumbered. In a word, cowards."

Dead cowards now, not that I feel bad about it. Technically, I didn't kill them, but I'm well aware that what just happened was the first time I've been involved with the death of humans. Well, technically fae, but up until now it's been a matter of ousting supernatural entities. Sometimes those entities have been posing as human, but that's not my problem. And it's not the same thing. On the other hand, those men thought nothing of delivering me into slavery and torture. And if it wasn't them, it was certainly men like them who ensnared Helen, Lily and Mitch. Yeah, good riddance.

"What do think magic should be used for?"

Esras seems more open now, as he relaxes into his chair. He gestures toward my arm. "Healing, for one thing. Pain relief and preventing disease. Used judiciously, that same energy can be useful for enhanced crop production, preventing or defeating certain types of blights. Lastly, defense against dark forces that can't otherwise be dealt with. And, of course, self-defense, but only when necessary."

I can't help but notice that Esras's perspective aligns perfectly with that of the witch community. Well, with the exception of those who stoop to using dark magic. But, hey, there are always going to be assholes.

The floor vibrates as an explosion sounds in the distance. The chamber we're sharing has so far muted most external sounds, so that must have been a big one.

"I guess it's still going on," I say.

Esras nods, not seeming surprised. "I don't imagine it's going to end anytime soon. At least not for long."

I look around the room again, curious. "Is there any way to keep an eye on things?"

He frowns. "I guess we could go back outside, or venture upstairs to look out the window, although I'm not sure either is a good idea."

Amusement bubbles up inside me. "No, I meant like TV or the internet." I almost add, "Silly," but I'm not sure how that would go over.

Esras shakes his head. "I'm sorry, those words don't mean anything to me."

It's an interesting aspect to this situation that, like Cade said, being able to visit this realm also allows me to understand the language. And speak it, apparently, as far as those around me are concerned. Except for those instances when there's no shared meaning.

Still, like an idiot, I try again. "You know, whatever you use to watch the news. Or shows."

Esras stares at me blankly, and again I fight the urge to giggle. "News," he says. "We have messengers to keep us informed, as needed. There's also the Special Council, which meets weekly. As for what you call "shows," I assume you must mean plays and performances, such as you might see in the company of others."

Okay, this is ridiculous. They have cities with apartment buildings, but they ride around on horses and fight with swords. Or magic. But, still. "We have screens," I say. "We use them to see the world, or to watch made up stories. We have big ones and little ones we keep in our pocket."

Esras frowns again. "You keep them in your pocket? So you can watch made up stories?"

"Sure. It's called internet and TV."

"And you watch these little screens alone," Esras says.

"Sure," I say proudly.

Esras nods thoughtfully this time, as he processes the information. "How strange."

I can't help it, and I burst out laughing.

Esras's face reddens. "I'm sorry. I guess that was rude of me."

"Actually, I guess it is a little strange. Now that you mention it." To Esras, it must seem weird as hell, but convening the Special Council to get the news strikes me as more than slightly archaic. Still, there's no sense in going there.

Another explosion thunders in the distance, this time rattling the room. It occurs to me that what we're experiencing might be some of those fireballs striking closer to home, although it's somehow more comforting to think it's just the Seelie continuing to be jerks. They can potentially be dealt with. Fireballs raining down from the sky is another matter altogether.

Esras gets up and goes to where one of the walls is lined with bookshelves and cabinets. He opens a cabinet and gets out two pewter mugs and a corked jug. He brings those to the sofa, sets them on the coffee table, and sits down beside me. Thank you, God.

Esras uncorks the jug and pours bright blue liquid into each of the mugs, filling them about a third of the way. "Trellberry wine," he says. "Ever had it?"

Weirdly, trellberries are always out of season on Earth. "Can't say that I have."

Esras's face reddens, presumably as he remembers how I've experienced visiting Faerie so far. He slides one of the mugs to me and picks up his own. "Of course. Well, to your health."

The wine is almost neon blue, looking more like something you'd paint with than drink. But what the hell. I lift my mug and say, "Cheers."

I take a sip and my taste buds go crazy. The wine is the perfect balance of sweetness and fruit, just dry enough, not too full and with undertones of what tastes like cherry, apple and strawberry. There's also just a hint of vanilla. And I thought the ale in Silvermist was good. Holy wow.

Now I just need Esras to heal me some more and I'd deeply consider never leaving this room.

"It's very brave, what you did," Esras says. "Coming back here, I mean."

I take another sip of my wine, trying not to chug. I really hope that jug is full. "I figured you'd think I'm insane."

He smiles. "Well, that did occur to me. Someone in your position would only come back for two reasons. She'd have to be either insane, or very committed to a cause. I took a leap of faith and made the assumption it's the latter."

"I came to help my friends," I say, "and I'm not leaving until I do."

Esras nods, keeping his eyes on mine. "That's what I assumed. Otherwise, you'd have stayed in your realm after helping that girl. Ellie, I believe her name was. I'm sorry, but I don't often enter the house."

Which I noticed, of course. And the feeling I get is that he's not okay with what's going on there. "Yes, Ellie. She's back with her family now."

"I'm glad to hear it."

I think again of that night, as I have so many times. My narrow escape from the Ferndelm house with Ellie, the alarm being suddenly sounded, and those men chasing after us on horses. If it hadn't been for Esras, I doubt we would have made it.

"Speaking of bravery," I say. "Thank you for what you did."

Esras shrugs, as if he did very little. "You're welcome."

I shake my head. "No, I mean it. You went up against your family. That can't have been easy."

Esras drinks some of his wine, his gaze going distant for a few moments. Finally, he speaks softly. "I've been at odds with them for a long time now. Ever since I was a child, essentially. Although, it wasn't until I got older that I fully understood. Nonetheless, what they do—what my people do—is wrong, and it has to stop."

Without meaning to, I drain what's left of my wine. It's just insanely good. Although, it might be the wine that allows me to ask, "But you still live with them? Your family, I mean."

"Not in the house, but for now I remain on the property of my ancestors. It's the Seelie way. Does that seem strange to you?"

If my parents kept slaves? You bet. Then again, it was Esras who helped to free us. He also kept those men from doing whatever they had planned for Ellie, and I'm pretty sure I know what that was. In many ways, Esras is doing more for helping those who are trapped by staying where he is. It's a conundrum, that's for sure, and maybe this isn't the time. Either way, clearly he's trying to help.

So, I just say, "A little. Yes."

Esras cocks his head. "But for many in your realm, I understand it's the same. Depending on cultural tradition. Isn't that so?"

Actually, I guess he's right. In some countries it's not unusual for adults to live at home, or for many generations to live beneath one roof. "I meant more like where I grew up," I say, so he understands where I'm coming from.

"I see." Esras lifts the jug, offering more. I nod, maybe a bit too eagerly, and he refills my mug and then his own. "So, you haven't remained with your family? How old were you when you left them?"

Oh boy. How to explain things? "Well, I sort of left home sooner than most. I was, well, eleven at the time." I suck back some wine. A little more than intended, actually. It would appear I'm a bit of a trellberry wine fiend, but I better take it easy. The stuff may not taste like it, but it packs a punch.

"Where did you go?"

Right, I kind of figured he'd ask. But then I remember what Cade told me when we first met, that the fae actually know of the supernatural creatures most humans refuse to believe in. "Have you heard of the Vamanec P'yrin?"

Esras nods. "The race of beings who can dwell within the bodies of others."

"Kind of like changelings."

His expression darkens. "Another practice that has to end, but yes. Except the Vamanec P'yrin don't create a double. Instead, they inhabit—" Esras stops and stares at me, his mug held aloft.

It wasn't what he intended, but I reach mine out to cheers him again. "Bingo. I got nabbed."

Esras recovers from his shock. "Your body was stolen? Is that what you're saying?"

I shrug. "Yep, that's the deal."

"But you somehow escaped? Where did you go?"

"Kind of a long story."

Esras shrugs. "Well, we have no place to go. And, as luck would have it, we seem to lack tiny screens."

I can't help but laugh. I bop my mug against his again, spilling a little this time. "Good one, Esras."

Yep, the trellberry wine is definitely kicking in. I really hope I can bring some of this stuff back with me. But he does have a point. We're basically stuck here for now. So, I tell him a condensed version of my seriously messed up life, while he listens intently.

I explain getting taken at the park on a summer night as a little girl, even as my sister stood just a few feet away. I tell him how Opal wanted to use my unique abilities as a veil witch against her longtime enemy, Paul, and how I psychically escaped to live within Julia for the years during which I would have been growing up. Even though I do my best to streamline, there's a lot to tell. We're on our third mug of wine by the time I get to how I accidentally found my way to Faerie, and how Grayson became interested in me, only to turn out to be Vintain in changeling form.

By the time I'm done, it occurs to me that Esras may know as much about me as anyone in the world. Of course, we're not in my world, but I've trusted so few people with this information. Part of that is because, in my realm, there are so few people I can tell. Non-magical humans would only think I'm insane. As for my witch counterparts, I've spent most of my time trying to fit in. It was a rocky start to begin with, and the last thing I want is to keep pointing out how different I am.

It also occurs to me that I might be insane trusting Esras this much. Does he know about the history Kezia shared with me and Cade? Not to mention the prophecy that one of Sativola's descendants would topple the Seelie from power? Those are his people, whether or not he agrees with what they do. Is it possible that I'm sitting beside my mortal enemy, someone who could soon want to see me destroyed?

Essentially, maybe I'm just drunk and should shut my mouth. But if there's anything to Julia's advice that, if you listen, your inner self will tell you the truth, then I know I can trust Esras with knowing who and what I am. In a sense, I'm betting my life on it, but I know in my heart that he's a good person. That he's kind and strong. And, yes, noble. The word suits him perhaps more than anyone I've encountered.

"Vintain," Esras says, snapping me out of it. "My father knows him, and my mother."

My pulse kicks up a notch. "My friend told me he's something called the High Mage. Is that true?"

Even though Esras already told me he knows about the person helping me, I still keep myself from using his name. After all, Cade must hate Esras. He's a Seelie noble, one of the same people Cade has devoted his life to defeating.

Esras lifts a knowing eyebrow, as if he can see right through me. "Your friend is right. Vintain is the High Mage."

"What does that mean?"

"The High Mage controls the realm's magic. It's been that way for hundreds of years. Ever since the Winter Court took the magic for themselves."

My heart starts hammering and I want to know more. Way more. But at the same time I don't want Esras to think that, after everything he's done, I'm just pumping him for information. I try to keep my voice casual. "And Queen Abarrane. Does your family know her too?"

Esras glances at the floor, as if he'd rather not admit it. "We're nobles, my father a duke and my mother a duchess. Both of my parents have roles within the Royal Court. Roles I'm not particularly proud of. I wish it were another way, but it's just the truth."

I know so little about how royal courts once functioned in my own realm, and I know nothing about how they work in Faerie. But if Esras's parents are part of that court, aren't there expectations that he will be too? It seems clear that he has no intention of participating. But, again, how well do I understand this world I've stepped into?

I can't help but dig further. "What's she like?"

"Dangerous," Esras says. "She's been in power for a very long time, and she's used to it. But that power can't last forever. She's well aware that time is running out, in more ways than one. Queen Abarrane is getting old, even for a fae."

His eyes meet mine long enough to make his point. Humans don't live long. Compared to the fae, we have the lifespans of mayflies.

"So, what does she plan to do?" Even as I ask the question, I fear I know the answer. I reach for my wine again, this time to beat back my nerves.

"Secure a new source of magical power, using her High Mage to find it for her. One that won't run out this time."

I shake my head. "Why? I mean, what's in it for them? Aren't they well off enough, or whatever it means to be rich in this realm? Why would they continue to do what they're doing?"

I gesture to the wall, meaning the scene we witnessed outside. The brutalization of the Unseelie people, the violence and the terror. And, of course, the potential for destroying the entire realm itself. Isn't it obvious that the place is shaking apart?

"Life," Esras says. "Immortality. Their forebears had that in your realm, and they want it back. Until then, Vintain will keep monopolizing the magic here to keep them alive."

In that moment, it all locks into place. Vintain is who I'm up against, and he always has been. And what he's been doing might also explain something I've wondered about since learning I'm a veil witch. Namely, what happened to all the others. Autumn told me it was because our kind faded over time, when people stopped believing in monsters. That we were no longer felt to be needed in our realm. But what if it's not that simple? What if we've been hunted to extinction in the search for one magical key?

"I need more wine," I say.

Esras fills my mug again. "Are you okay?"

My expression must betray the revelation I just experienced. Am I wrong? Possibly, but my gut tells me otherwise.

"I'm okay," I say.

Which is a total lie. I'm completely freaked out.

But this one I'm keeping to myself. There's no one else I'm discussing it with but Autumn. How Vintain hasn't yet found her, I can't imagine. The only thing I can think is that he's been limited by his own magic. In our realm, he was spying through a changeling called Grayson, the real Grayson having been held captive in Faerie. And that changeling heard about me somehow through Grimoire, but not my sister. Pure luck, but how long will that luck hold? Isn't it only a matter of time before Vintain discovers that there's another veil witch?

Esras watches me, not saying anything as I think things through. It takes me a few moments even to remember where I am. But for now, there's nothing to be done about what I just realized. I bring my gaze back to his.

Maybe it's the wine, or maybe I'm just worn out, but I need to understand what I'm dealing with. My fate is one thing, my sister's another.

"Why are you helping me?"

He doesn't look away. "Because I swore an oath."

"To who?"

"To my sister."

"Fashenan?"

Esras's eyes widen. "How do you know her name?"

I consider telling him that I've seen her ghost, that she led me toward something she very much wanted me to see. I decide I should probably keep that to myself for now.

I keep it simple. "I know what happened," I say.

How I learned that, Esras doesn't ask. He must assume I found out through either Helen or Lily, but I guess he decides it doesn't matter.

He nods, and then continues. "That's when everything changed for me. When Fashenan died, I started questioning everything. Who we were. What we valued. What mattered, what didn't, and what was acceptable. I decided that her death wouldn't be in vain, and that it was up to me to see her purpose through. That I'd act in her name when the time came."

"And do you believe the time is now?" I say.

"I do. I'm sure of it."

"Why were you there tonight?" Despite the fact that he very well might have saved my life, I still need to know how he found me again.

Esras doesn't hesitate. "I was following those men. Yes, with the intention of putting an end to them. I plan to do the same for the rest of their kind. However, the timing was… fortunate."

Yeah, no kidding, and relief washes over me at his words. Instinctively, I know he's telling the truth.

When I remain silent, Esras says, "Did you suspect something other than coincidence?"

His gaze remains on mine, open and steady. There's no resentment in his voice. Just curiosity.

"I wasn't sure what to think. I mean, when you just showed up like that."

Esras nods. "It's totally understandable that you'd have your guard up. You've been through a lot. More than most people would likely survive."

I sip my wine, thinking about what he said. He's right, somehow I have managed to survive so much more than I ever could have imagined. In fact, most of the things I've survived are also things I couldn't have imagined. But I have to survive this too if I'm going to save Julia.

As we continue sitting together without speaking, I realize it's grown quiet outside. The echoes of violence have faded away. I also realize that I too am starting to fade. So much has happened tonight. It feels like a lifetime of events have taken place within just the past few hours.

As if sensing my thoughts, Esras says, "You should get some rest."

He moves to get up, but I place my hand on his leg. "What about you?"

He nods toward the chairs across from us. "I'll be fine resting right there. Please don't worry about me."

Without thinking about it, I draw him toward me. I know that if I think about it, I'll stop. My pulse escalates as I raise my lips to his, wondering if I'll be accepted, and if he feels the same way.

Esras closes his eyes and leans in toward me. His lips, soft and full, brush mine gently at first, but the kiss soon grows more urgent. I part my lips and his tongue dances with my own. When a moment ago, I felt myself fading, suddenly I'm on fire. Heat ripples through every fiber of my body, building and spreading fast. My heart pounds within my chest, and I let out a moan as Esras's kisses travel to the underside of my chin and then my neck. He keeps going lower, and I arch my back, the urge to thrust nearly impossible to resist. I want his hands inside my shirt. I want to peel off his clothes while he does the same to me.

But then, as if knowing what I truly need, Esras brings his lips to mine again. He kisses me softly once more, and then draws away. He keeps his arms around me, holding on as my heartbeat starts to slow. Gently, he trails his fingers through my hair. Little by little, I start falling into a lull. Part of me wonders if it's magic, while part of me suspects I'm just exhausted. And that Esras knows this just isn't the time. We've been through too much. Finally, he eases us down to where we lay side by side.

He speaks softly. "Sleep, Cassie. Let yourself sleep."

He keeps his arms wrapped around me and I feel myself once again starting to fade. Finally, I surrender to sleep, as Esras holds me in his arms.

CHAPTER 10

I'm in my old house, the one I knew as a child, and it's early morning as I make my way downstairs. I cross through the empty living room, rubbing my eyes and thinking how strange the light is today. It flickers at the windows, casting an orange glow across the wall. In the kitchen, I look up to where my mother stands at the counter. She has her back to me. She's thin, wearing a dress she used to wear long ago. Her dark hair still flows to her shoulders, not yet streaked with gray. Music plays from the radio she keeps in there, pop rock from when she was a girl. She doesn't turn from where she's preparing breakfast, but she must have heard me come in. Or maybe she just senses me behind her.

"Would you like some juice, sweetheart?"

"Yes, mama."

She gets a glass from the cabinet, and I watch as she fills it with the bright orange liquid. It's the same color I saw in the living room, and my eyes go to the windows again where that same light still flickers.

"Mama, why is the sky that color?"

My mother looks at the window too, her back still turned to me. "That's because it's a new day, sweetie. Go have a look."

I have no idea what she means, but she sounds happy. I walk to the door and swing it open, excited to look outside. But my neighborhood is gone, replaced by a city street on fire. Entire buildings are encased in flame. Smoke spirals up toward the sky, as a shrill alarm pierces the air. I cover my ears and stare as men on horseback charge through the streets, galloping over outstretched bodies. They have bone-white skin and long white hair. They're tall and muscled, with eyes of purple, bright orange and green.

I open my mouth to scream, but then feel my mother next to me. She reaches down and gently runs her fingers through my hair. She says, "Isn't it beautiful?"

"I'm scared, mama."

I raise my eyes to see Raakel looking down at me, a grin spreading across her face.

"Don't be scared, sweetie," she says. "You made this happen."

I sit bolt upright, gasping for air as my heart hammers in my chest. I look around, completely disoriented. I'm in a dimly lit room with a table and chairs. I see shelves of books and a map on the wall. Then it comes back to me— the soldiers, the fires, the crowds, facing off against those men and Esras bringing me here. Damn, no wonder I had that dream. One that, no doubt, will take its place in my personal nightmare hall of fame.

I look around again, but there's no sign of him. There's a glass of water on the table beside the sofa, one that Esras must have left there. I reach for it with a shaky hand. The water is cool, and very much needed after my little trellberry wine binge. I drain the glass in a series of thirsty gulps, suddenly remembering more.

Oh, my God. What did I do last night? Did we...? No, we didn't. I would have, that's for sure, but Esras showed restraint. I'm not quite sure how to feel about that. Was I rejected? Um, yeah, maybe a little. But maybe trellberry wine doesn't have quite the same effect on Esras, who had the common sense to know it probably wasn't the best idea. In fact, maybe he chose not to take advantage of me when I was wasted, which only makes me feel better about him.

My head snaps up at the sound of voices coming from above. What I hear is muted and faint, but calm. Just men and women talking. Although, I can't hear what they're saying.

I cross the room, ease the door open, and go out into the hall. There's no sign of Esras, but the voices grow louder. I keep walking, trying to listen as I come to the stairs and start to climb, staying as quiet as possible. I hear a woman say my name, and I freeze on the steps. I listen, making out a little more this time, as a man says "veil witch." My heart starts beating fast as I try to understand. Has Esras been taken, and am I walking into a trap? I'm just not sure, and I consider turning back to hide in the room where I slept. Maybe I can get that back door to slide open, and make a run for it outside.

Then I recognize one of the voices. It's Esras, I'm sure. "Understandably, she was exhausted," he says. "I thought it best to let her sleep."

Okay, I still don't know what's going on, but I start to calm down. I highly doubt he'd be discussing my need for rest with anyone intending us harm. I keep climbing the stairs, enter a hall, and come to a door opening onto a room where people sit around a table. Suddenly, I realize where I am. It's the same room where Cade and I met with Revlen. Sure enough, she sits at the table, along with some of those who were with her the last time, and it dawns on me that we just spent the night beneath the Gilded Gargoyle.

Then my mouth drops open at seeing Cade sitting beside Esras. Wait. Esras is a Seelie noble. Cade is, well, whatever he is. The rest of them are Unseelie rebels. What the hell?

At that moment, Cade spots me. He jumps up, a happy grin spreading across his face as he walks toward me. "There you are!"

I stand frozen, with my eyes flicking back and forth. And, I'm pretty sure, my mouth hanging open.

Cade wraps me in a completely unexpected hug, squeezing me hard enough that it hurts. "I was worried sick about you last night! I was freaking out, looking all over the place."

Suddenly, I can't help but feel guilty. I mean, I did look for him, but he could have been killed ten times over while I sucked back trellberry wine and thought about jumping Esras's bones. I manage to find my voice, a blush rising to my face. "I'm okay," I say. "We were, um, downstairs."

This doesn't seem to bother Cade at all. In fact, he couldn't seem more happy. "I know! Esras told us. Thank God he found you or who knows what might have happened?"

I look around again, still shell-shocked. "You guys know each other?"

It's a stupid question since, obviously, they do. It's just that when Esras said he knew about my friend, the half-blood thief, I thought he meant that he *knew about my friend, the half-blood thief.* It never occurred to me that Esras actually knew Cade. Especially since, if I understand things correctly, they should be trying to kill each other.

It's Revlen who answers my question. "We do, indeed," she says. She doesn't add more, but she smiles while bringing her golden eye to bear on me. "How are you this morning?"

I almost forgot how stunning she is, with her honey blonde hair, high cheekbones and full lips. On her, the eye patch seems like a sexy accessory.

It's not an easy question to answer. I decide on, "A little... disoriented."

By which I mean, I left one realm to visit two more, witnessed a battle, found out that I'm notorious in Scintillia, and bunked down drunk with the same Seelie noble who helped me escape from Faerie the first time. Not to mention, felt pretty much fine about having sex with him. Kind of a busy night.

"Of course," Revlen says. "It stands to reason. Would you like some coffee?"

97

Thank God some things appear to be universal to all three realms, coffee being one of them. How that came to be, I can't imagine, but I'm not about to argue. "Coffee sounds great, actually."

Revlen gestures to an open spot beside Cade, where he's taken his place back at the table. Revlen fills a cup of coffee from a carafe. "Milk and sugar?" she says.

Come to think of it, I haven't yet seen what a cow might look like in Faerie. Hopefully, nothing like a golork. "Yes, please."

Revlen brings me the coffee and then takes her seat again. She gestures to the people I haven't yet met. There are just two men this time, and one other woman. One of the men has very dark skin and jet black hair, while the other appears to be what I'd think of as Middle Eastern, although that frame of reference must mean nothing here. The woman is fair, with short auburn hair and blue eyes. Even seated, I can tell she's taller than the men. She wears a tank top revealing broad shoulders and muscular arms.

"This is Ecubon, Tonorf and Verin," Revlen says, indicating them in order of seating.

I nod to each of them, not quite sure what to say. *Nice to meet you. Now let's go kick some Seelie ass?* Actually, it's probably about right, except for the strange aspect of having Esras at the table.

Revlen breaks the ice. "Cade tells me you came back to save another one of your friends. I have to say, we're quite impressed with what you've managed to accomplish."

Pointing out that, technically, Ellie wasn't my friend feels like splitting hairs. But I have to set the record straight. On top of which, I really don't want them to overestimate my abilities, which have proven to be extremely unreliable in this realm. "Esras helped us escape. If it wasn't for him, we never would have made it."

Revlen nods. "We're aware of how he assisted you."

Oh, of course. I suddenly realize that's how she knew to begin with, and could tell Cade about it. The information didn't reach her through some mysterious informant within her rebel network. Esras told her. Well, damn. This place may be strange as hell, but it's never boring.

Revlen reads my expression correctly. "That's right. Esras has been a sympathizer for some time. As you can imagine, he assisted you at great personal risk."

Her words remind me of something I've wondered about a few times. But it's not like I ever thought I'd see Esras again, and with all that went on last night I forgot to ask him.

I turn to Esras. "Wait? Doesn't your family know you helped us?"

I mean, how can they not, all things considered?

He shakes his head. "There were no actual witnesses, and we were too far away from my father's men for them to see us clearly. On top of that, even if they had their suspicions, they'd be very hesitant voicing them to my father."

Right, in that respect, things here aren't much different than in my realm. People fear the rich and powerful. No one wants to tell them what they don't want to hear, not if it means their job. Or, possibly, their head.

Then something else occurs to me. "But we escaped on horseback."

Esras lifts an eyebrow. "And you can imagine how upset the guards were to later discover that someone had released them all from the stable. Presumably, the same two women who used one to escape."

I lift an appreciative eyebrow of my own. "Well played."

He nods, just a hint of a smile tugging at his lip. "Thank you."

Revlen is grinning, I notice. As are the others at the table. It would seem approval is unanimous when it comes to pulling one over on Luchtane Ferndelm's thugs.

"True, Esras helped you escape the property and get across the Barrens," Revlen says. "But it was you who broke a changeling spell. Which, as I'm sure Cade told you, is quite an interesting development."

I shrug and say, "I take it that's a new one."

Revlen studies me for a moment, and the feeling I get is that she's confused why I'm not more impressed with myself. But, hey, I've been pulling off impossible stunts since I was a child. Most of the time, I find my unique abilities more annoying than impressive. After all, without them I might have had a normal life.

"Yes, that's absolutely a new one," Revlen says. "As in, no one has ever undone a mage's changeling magic."

My head swivels back and forth between her and Esras. I focus on him. "Wait, I thought…"

Esras stares back at me as he takes a sip of coffee.

I try again. "I just figured you could all do that sort of thing. I mean, it's fae magic."

Esras sets his cup down. "Create changelings? Definitely not. Only a mage would hold that kind of power. And right now, there's essentially only one mage."

I let that one sink in for a moment. "So you can't undo that kind of spell?"

"I'm afraid most can't achieve that either," Esras admits.

That answers another one of my questions. I've wondered why he wouldn't help someone like Ellie until someone like me came along. But he had no way to return her to the human realm. In a place that has so far made no sense, at least some things are starting to make sense.

"Okay, let's circle back to that other thing," I say. "Why can only mages create changelings?"

Why do I have the weirdest feeling that I know the answer?

A moment later proves me right, when Esras says, "Because only mages have access to that level of magic."

Yep, bingo. "Can we talk about that? Because I found this magical globe thing in that house where I was being held—" Realizing what I'm saying, I stop and add, "Sorry, Esras. But I found it in your father's study."

Esras lifts both eyebrows this time. "You gained access to the Amulus? That's not—" He shakes his head and tries again. "Apparently, it is possible, for you. For anyone else it wouldn't be possible."

I realize that everyone is staring at me. I just keep stepping into more and more fae shit, don't I?

"Don't you have access to the, what's it called again?"

"Amulus," Esras says. "And no, I don't have access."

This is turning out to be the morning when I point out all the things Esras can't do. Sorry, Esras.

"So, how does it work? The magical thingy? The network? Whatever it is."

Again, everyone stares at me, although I'm pretty sure I know why.

"That's what we're trying to figure out," Verin says. It's the first time one of Revlen's associates has spoken. Way to kick things off, Verin, by pointing out I'm a total idiot. Then again, she doesn't look like a woman to pull punches.

I hate to do this to Esras again, but I sort of have to. "Even *you* don't know how it works?"

Esras shrugs, but thankfully that smile plays on his lips again. Right, he's humble to begin with, so he's not exactly threatened by my outing him as not being all powerful. "Well, you're right about it being a network. And I understand the underpinnings, if not all of the intricacies. That's because only those who created it fully understand those aspects."

"Those with the right level of access," I say.

"Exactly. You're getting the picture," Esras says. "The system was laid in place over a thousand years ago, by Vintain's High Mage predecessors."

Wait. This crap has been going on for a thousand years?

Another one of Revlen's people joins the conversation. This time, Ecubon. "Following the War of the Courts," he says, understandably perceiving my stunned silence as confusion. "Have you heard of those?"

So, there's no doubt that I was discussed before making my entrance since, obviously, Ecubon knows I'm human. Otherwise, he wouldn't be asking the question. "The war fought to gain control of the magic."

"Exactly," he says. "I wasn't sure how much you might know about fae history."

Clearly, he means only to keep me in the loop. "Not very much," I say. "Thank you."

Ecubon nods and Esras continues.

"Before that time, all fae had some level of magic. Some more than others, but it had nothing to do with whether you were of Seelie or Unseelie ancestry. And, by the way, many believe that at one time there was no such distinction made between our people. I, for one, agree. As do many other Seelie. It's not the Seelie in general who are despised by the Unseelie. In fact, it's a very small ruling minority."

I have no doubt that Esras realizes he's part of that minority, and it's sad to think he'd be despised by most he's trying to help. At the same time, I understand. He can't both openly work with the resistance and remain a valuable asset. At least, not yet.

This time, it's the guy next to Ecubon who chimes in. Tonorf. "Many feel it's an entirely artificial ethnic classification," he says. "One created by the prolonged period of cultural isolation following the war."

Definitely more helpful information to fill in some of the blanks. "So, basically, those who gained control of the power not only kept it to themselves, they kept to themselves."

"Exactly," Verin says. "Well put. In other words, it's much more a matter of social hierarchy than anything intrinsically biological."

Okay, I'm starting to like her better.

Esras continues. "Once the power was seized, the High Mages devised a system whereby only the Seelie would have access to it. Each Seelie noble house was given an object like the one you discovered. That object, what we call an Amulus, channels magic from the main source."

"Kind of like electricity," Cade says. "There's the main turbine generator, and then there are conductors and transformers, all working to distribute power. Eventually, that power is stepped down until it reaches an electrical panel in a house."

His eyebrows arch proudly following his explanation. God, he really is such a nerd.

"But houses have outlets where we plug into the power," I say. I turn to Esras again, but he gets where I'm going. He holds out his hand to show me a gold ring with a deep red stone.

"All Seelie wear a charmed object of some nature," he says. "In my case, it's this ring. For others, it might be a pendant or a bracelet. The objects differ, but they all serve the same purpose."

"Hang on," I say. "So, if all the Unseelies took away all of these objects, they'd hold the power?"

Esras shakes his head. "It's not that simple. For one thing, it's quite difficult for someone without power to take an object from someone holding it. Essentially, one side remains magically unarmed. Add to that, to make a difference, they'd have to somehow gain control of them all at the same time. Which is, of course, logistically impossible. And, if needed, the same magic can be redirected to another object."

I speak softly as I get the picture. "So, even if they got power, they wouldn't be able to keep it." Damn, it's really insidious. Kind of ingenious, but still totally warped. Then I remember what Cade said before. "Where's the generator?"

Esras doesn't hesitate. "Within the palace, I'm sure."

Interesting. Because that's exactly where I'm going at the very first opportunity. How I'm going to pull that off, I have no idea, but it's the only way to free Julia.

"But we're getting ahead of ourselves," Revlen says. "We know we can't cut the source of that power. Not yet, anyway. But we do know that same power has started to destabilize. It's becoming more and more unpredictable."

"Why?" I say. "I mean, why after all of this time?"

Even as I ask, a chill ripples down my spine. Deep within myself, I know the answer. I felt it in that moment when the ley line reached out to me. Clearly, she's chosen this time to finally fight back. Almost as if she's been waiting for something. Or someone.

"We're not sure," Revlen says. "All we know is that it's happening. And, right now, we need to hold steady. The time to strike might be imminent. Merely a matter of weeks, perhaps days. We can only gauge that by the intervals during which magical power eludes the Seelie grasp. However, one thing seems clear. Those intervals keep growing more frequent, and they keep getting longer."

Suddenly, it dawns on me that we haven't talked about my plan to rescue Julia. It seems almost assumed that I've come to join this rebel cause. That's not why I'm here.

"Listen, I'm sorry." I look around the table. "But I'm wondering if we might not be on the same page. I get what's going on here, and I care. I really do. But I need to help my friend."

A moment passes, and then Revlen nods. She keeps her penetrating gaze fixed on me. "Cade told us why you came back. We hope to help you in any way we can."

I start to relax a little. "Thank you."

"But your friend is within the palace," Revlen says.

When she doesn't say more, I nod. "Yes, she is."

"And to get near her, you'd have to single-handedly slip past all of their defenses. And, after doing so, you'd need to confront, and defeat, the same people currently hunting you down."

My confidence definitely starts to slip. When Revlen puts it that way, it becomes obvious that it would be a suicide mission. Which is not my intention. Getting killed or captured wouldn't help Julia. In fact, it would only guarantee that she never gets rescued.

I hesitate, but then ask, "So, what were you thinking?"

"I understand your feelings," Revlen says. "Believe me, I do. This isn't your fight. It's not why you came here. I respect that."

I breathe out a sigh of relief. "Thank you."

She nods. "At the same time, we all have stakes in this game. Why we want things to change depends on every story involved, each of them different. I'm sure you understand that. Not all are looking toward the greater good. Some want change for more personal reasons. And I understand that too. It's perfectly natural."

I'm not sure where she's going, but there's no doubt that the more I'm around Revlen, the more I respect her. Like her, in fact. She's clearly a strong and intelligent woman. A leader, willing to fight for what she believes in, while accepting that others might have different beliefs.

"I'm sure that's true," I say.

"You're also a valuable asset. Whether that's how you view yourself doesn't change anything. Clearly, the High Mage thinks so, or he wouldn't be doing what he's been doing."

Revlen keeps her tone dispassionate, putting no guilt on me. Still, her words carry the weight of the truth. People suffered last night because of me. They died because of me. It's a horrifying realization, but it's true. That's why Vintain brought his men into that neighborhood to begin with.

They were looking for me. That's why they burned buildings and terrorized those people.

My gut twists as this reality keeps sinking in. "I understand," I say, softly. The fact is, Revlen's understated words just hugely shifted my perspective.

"So, what I'd like to do, if you'll allow me, is to keep you safe."

I look back at Revlen, not sure what she means. "What would that involve?"

"For the time being, I think it would be best if we took you someplace distant. Someplace where Queen Abarrane and Vintain won't be searching for you. By that, I mean, out of Scintillia."

I shake my head with confusion. "I don't understand. Where would I go? For how long?"

"I suspect not long," Revlen says. "But we have to be careful. It's too dangerous for everyone right now if you remain here. Vintain will only increase his patrols and inspections. Last night was just the beginning. Of that, I feel sure. What I'm proposing is that we take you to the Mollern. Specifically, to Longmeadow."

Cade perches forward, nearly spilling his coffee. "Wait? Are you sure about this?"

"As much as I'm sure about anything," Revlen says.

Cade runs his hand through his hair, as he looks around the table and then back to Revlen. "But they're not involved. That's why they went there to begin with, to get away."

Revlen nods, acknowledging Cade's point, but then she says, "We're all involved, whether we like it or not. I spoke to Dabria last week."

Cade's eyes grow wide, his forehead starting to glisten. "Wait. She came here?"

"She did. She came at the request of her father, who wanted us to know that their people have pledged their support. I'm sorry, Cade. But they're willing to take the risk, and I feel we have no choice."

Cade's eyes shift to me. And, for the first time, I get the feeling that he wishes we'd never met.

CHAPTER 11

We wait until night to ride out. There are four of us, Esras, Cade, Revlen and me. That Revlen chooses to join us, rather than sending one of her charges, surprises me a little. But I guess, like she said, I'm a valuable asset. So, maybe she feels she should take responsibility for my protection. Then again, maybe by traveling with me, she hopes to learn more about what makes me tick. I can tell she's curious.

As for Cade, I'm relieved to see that he's no longer upset. Clearly, he didn't like the idea of us going to Dabria's village. He stayed quiet after our meeting, and then went back to Silvermist for part of the afternoon. To take care of a few things, he said at the time, although I really think he just needed to get past his anger. Now, he seems fine, so I guess he's at least resigned himself to the plan.

We leave the city by way of alleys and smuggler's routes, before long approaching the Barrens, that expanse of white gleaming like a bone in the moonlight. My stomach plunges at the sight of that place where I've scrambled for my life several times. I can't help but ask. "Aren't we using one of the tunnels?"

"We should be okay," Esras says. "There aren't any wards to trip on this side of the city."

Which I guess makes sense. The Seelie don't care if the Unseelie wander into the Barrens. Why would they? It only matters if one of their changeling or half-blood captives tries to escape.

Still, I look at the sky. "What about the dragon?"

"The dragon is only set loose when one of the noble houses sounds an alarm," Revlen says.

Which brings to mind that thing Cade said before, about dragons normally being unaggressive, and that seeing one is considered a good omen. "Where is it kept the rest of the time?"

Esras and Revlen exchange glances. "You wouldn't like it," Revlen says. "Not from what we hear."

She leaves it at that, and I don't press. I guess it's just another thing I'll learn about at some point. Right now, as we ride our horses forward into the open, it might be better to remain quiet.

Despite what Esras said about there being no wards, we remain watchful as we ride. Even the horses seem wary, with their heads raised and their ears lifted. Still, it's the first time I've been through the Barrens when I wasn't terrified, and I gaze out across the vast and empty stretch where ivory ash lays like a blanket of snow. A fireball streaks across the sky, casting a fiery glow upon flakes twirling down. It's a strange feeling, and not one I expected, but I can't help thinking it's beautiful in a surreal way. Sad, I know. A dead and forgotten land, but striking all the same in its eerie otherworldliness.

What lends even more strangeness to the moment is that I'm taking everything in while astride a tall and powerful horse. His name is Andor, and he rocks gently beneath me, his strong neck and noble head raised high. I think about that moment, not long ago, when I wished for a normal life. Right now, I'm not so sure. I've endured a lot, and I'm soon to go up against even more. Still, in this moment, I'm guiding a stallion across an alien landscape, one no human sees of their own free will. The land before me gleams white and colorful fireballs streak across a night full of stars. I'm surrounded by silence, except for the soft sound of hoofbeats against the ground. Yes, it's strange, and in many ways desolate. Still, there's only one word I can think of to describe it. Magical.

*

We ride slowly, both to avoid being noticed and to keep from tiring the horses. All the same, we soon reach the other side and enter the forest from where I've come and gone in the past. The horses snort and lower their heads, their ears relaxing now that we're out of the open. Those of us atop them appear less wary as well, and we relax more in our saddles. I turn to Revlen as she rides up beside me. "What's this place called?" It's never occurred to me as having a name before, but of course it must.

"Lanisan," she says. "They say it was once lush and beautiful. Abundant with life of every kind. Not all of it timid, of course."

"People used to hunt here," Esras says. "Hundreds of years ago. Now they can only hunt in the fields and forests we stock."

I look around at the trees with their trunks of exotic hues. Even by moonlight, I see purple, peach, pink and yellow. I remember spotting that frozen blue bud weeks ago, looking as if it had just started to sprout. Could it really have remained that way for hundreds of years?

"Could it still come back?"

Esras nods. "Possibly. We like to think it's more in a state of suspension than truly dead."

"The magic resource depletion has the greatest effect on areas immediately surrounding the city," Revlen explains. "That's because the energy is being diverted. Farther out, it's not as bad. Nothing like what it once was, but at least it's… Well, you'll see."

It's hard to gauge time, but it feels like about an hour before we leave the forest and emerge again beneath a sea of stars. With no light pollution this time, or fireballs streaking down, what I see is utterly stunning. I suspect I'm seeing the night sky like our ancestors did long ago. Before us, the land appears to go on forever, with tall grass waving gently in the moonlight.

"This is the Mollern," Revlen explains. "The village we're going to is out there."

"Is it far?"

"Far enough."

As more hours pass, my entire body starts to ache. I don't know if anyone else is feeling it, but I really need to stop. I can see where Revlen and Esras might be used to this, since they must have grown up on horses. To them, this probably feels like a leisurely ride through the country. Cade, on the other hand, has to be hurting too. Although, if he is, he doesn't say as much. Then again, I haven't made my discomfort known either.

Finally, Esras points to where something glimmers up ahead. "Let's make camp there," he says.

His eyes proved sharp, since what he saw turns out to be a pond. Suddenly, it occurs to me why we might have kept pushing on. We brought food and water for ourselves. The silly horses, on the other hand, didn't think to pack a thing.

At long last, I hop off Andor, who snorts and gives me a sorrowful look. It's almost like I can hear him thinking, *You would have let me die of thirst, wouldn't you?*

I avert my eyes since the answer, my poor Andor, is that until now I didn't think of you.

*

We make camp beneath the stars. No tents. Just the blankets we brought laid out on the ground. But it's dry, and a warm breeze blows through the air of what would be a winter night back in my realm. We eat by the fire, a dinner of fruit, cheese and smoked meat. When we've finished, Esras leaves to check on the horses and Revlen goes to lie down. Sleep sounds good to me too, but it's the first time I've been alone with Cade since last night, and I want to make sure things are okay.

Until now, I've never asked, but something tells me it's time to know. After all, like Revlen said, we all have different stakes in this game. For Cade, I'm sure that's Dabria.

"What's she like?" I say.

Cade looks up from where he's gazing into the fire. "Is it that obvious?"

"That you're thinking about her? I get the feeling you usually are."

He takes a sip of water from his canteen. "Sometimes I try not to, but it doesn't seem to work."

In a way, I envy his worry. I can't say I've ever really felt that way about someone. Even with Phoenix, I always remained a little distant, always felt afraid to fully commit.

"She must be really special," I say.

"She is. I'm sure you'll like her."

That I'm going to meet her is another thing I didn't expect, but it also means I'm placing her in danger.

"Where did you two meet?"

"In Faerie," Cade says, making me laugh.

"Good one. Care to be a little more specific?"

"It wasn't long after I started coming over, at the Festival of Titania. They have it every spring in Gorgedden. It's sort of a big deal there. There's music, beer and games. That kind of stuff."

"Sounds fun," I say. "Not something I imagined saying about Faerie."

Cade laughs. "Yeah, exactly. The place is a little short on good times. Anyway, half the reason I went was to try unloading some stuff I'd stolen from the Seelie. I didn't sell much, but it definitely made a good impression. The Unseelie don't worry about the whole half-blood thing. They don't really care one way or the other. But a half-blood who sneaks into Seelie houses and lives to tell about it? That's a different thing entirely."

"Cade the rock star."

He grins. "That's me. So, I fell in with a crowd. We were drinking, talking, dancing, all that. Suddenly I looked up and there was this girl. Beautiful brown hair, big brown eyes, the whole package. You know?"

"Something tells me you were just as interested in the package as the big brown eyes."

Cade laughs again. "Aw, you don't think I'm that kind of guy, do you?"

I give him a nudge. "Actually, I don't."

"Didn't think so, but good. So, yeah, that was Dabria. We started talking and she'd never met a half-blood before. She had all these questions about Silvermist and the human realm."

"Cade, inter-dimensional man of mystery."

Cade nudges me this time. "You got it. For her, it was love at first sight."

"Oh, I'm sure. And you were as cool as can be, I bet. Regaling her with your adventures, so you could have your way with the innocent young lass."

"Man, you know me. We spent half the night talking, and half the night dancing. Before I knew it, the festival was closing down."

"Did you kiss her? I hope you kissed her."

Cade laughs. "You're the worst audience. You know that, right?"

"I pride myself on it."

"So, yeah. Like you probably guessed, we began seeing each other. I started coming over more and more. Which is risky, obviously. Back then, Dabria's family lived in the city. Her father moved them out to the Mollern later when things kept getting worse."

"Smart man."

"Yeah, he is. You'll like him too, and Dabria's mom."

A few moments pass in silence as we stare into the fire. Finally, I say, "So, I don't understand. What happened? It sounds like you two were falling in love."

Cade sighs. "That's just it, we were. As in, crazy, want to spend your life together, in love. As in, want to get married and have kids, in love. And what were we going to do with that? I can't stay here, and she can't leave…"

Cade sighs again. He picks up a stick and pokes at the fire, sending sparks swirling into the night.

"Did you stop seeing her?"

"That's the problem. I can't. The whole thing is just a recipe for heartbreak. It's tearing me up."

God, we know so little about each other, and here we are putting our lives in each other's hands. Without thinking about it, I shift closer and I rest my head on his shoulder. We sigh together this time.

"So, what do you actually do in the human realm? Do you, like, have a job?"

"Uber driver," Cade says.

I don't know why, but it makes me laugh.

"What?"

"I don't know. I guess I sort of pictured you as a game developer. Or a computer programmer."

"Why, because I'm such a nerd?"

A smile spreads across my face. "Kind of, yeah."

"Well, I can't exactly keep regular hours."

"No, it makes sense. Ignore me."

"Not an option. You keep getting into trouble."

I laugh again. "True. I have a knack for that. What would you do if, I don't know, things changed?"

A few seconds pass as Cade considers. "Move here, I guess. Stop stealing. Get married. From there, I'm not sure. I've always liked being around people, and I know a good beer when I taste one. Dabria likes music and she's smart about money. Maybe we could run a pub together."

"That sounds nice," I say. And it does. I picture Cade standing proudly behind his bar, while his pretty wife goes from table to table checking on the customers and making them laugh. I imagine little curly-haired versions of Cade, with adorable pointy ears, running around and causing mischief.

Cade sighs again. "I guess it will all work out somehow," he says. "It has to."

Exactly, I think. Somehow, it all has to be worked out.

CHAPTER 12

I wake up as something tightens around my wrists. By the time I even open my eyes, I'm lifted into the air. Two men look down at me, one at my feet and the other at my bound hands. Both of them have long hair and beards. Both of them are shirtless, with heavily muscled chests and arms. In the time it takes me to scream out a, "Hey! What the *fuck!*" I'm flipped upright and dropped into Andor's saddle, to which my wrists are immediately lashed with blindingly efficient speed. In about ten seconds, I just went from being sound asleep to sitting roped to my horse.

The men back away, their expressions grim. But it's not their faces that has my eyes bugging out. It's their bodies. Particularly, the lower half of their bodies, which are also entirely naked. Not to mention entirely horse. Centaurs? Come on! Nobody thought to mention centaurs? Are you freaking kidding me? And what the hell is it with Faerie? Does anyone come through here without being captured for something? I mean, seriously, what's the deal?

My dizziness at being flipped through the air like pizza dough starts to clear. I look around to see that I was the last out of the four of us to find herself in this situation. Why, I have no idea. Maybe I just sleep more soundly. Either way, Cade, Esras and Revlen have also been manhandled similarly. Horsehandled? The correct verb escapes me at the moment. They look back at me gravely, from where they sit lashed to their saddles. I open my mouth to speak just as one of the centaurs yells out a command. I have no idea what he says, but evidently our horses do, since they set off at a healthy trot.

There appear to be six centaurs, three riding at the front and three at the rear, leaving us in the middle. Wait, do centaurs ride? Not really, I guess. I mean, the ride is built in. Again, my mind reels at how weird this is. Wait, am I dreaming? I pull against my ropes, making my wrists burn. Nah, dreams don't chafe. Besides, this is too strange to be a dream.

I look over at Esras. "I assume this can't be good."

"Probably not," he says.

At least there's a 'probably' in his response. Not much hope to go on, but I'll take what I can get.

I lower my voice to a whisper. "What about your magic?"

Esras wiggles his fingers, from where they're bound to his saddle. Oh, great. His ring is gone. Either the horsemen are very well informed, or naturally suspicious. Either way, shit.

As for my own magic, while I felt it returning last night once we got past the Barrens, now it feels blocked again. I can only guess it has something to do with the centaurs. Guessing my train of thought, Esras nods toward those riding at the front. "In their hair," he says. "Blocking wards."

I look to see that each of them wears a glowing green stone woven into his hair. They don't mess around, these centaurs. But what is it with everyone stepping on each other's magic in this realm? And there I was thinking humans were possessive.

"Where are they taking us?"

"Well, not in the direction of Scintillia," Esras says. "So that part's good."

How he can tell out here in the middle of nowhere, I have no idea. Still, I figure he's probably right. This is his realm, after all.

I get jostled and almost say, "I have to pee," but decide against it. First of all, it will only make things worse. Secondly, it's undignified. And it's not like there's anything to do about it, other than call out to the centaurs at the front. *Excuse me, Mr. Centaur? I need to pee.* Um, no. This sucks.

I look around again, trying not to appear as angry as I feel. "Why didn't anyone mention centaurs?"

Revlen takes this one. "They're not typically an aggressive people."

Okay, so they're considered people. Good to know. "This seems kind of aggressive. Or is it me?"

"I agree," Revlen says. "This would seem somewhat aggressive."

Glad to hear we're on the same page. "So, how to explain it?"

"Well, they can get a little resentful of others crossing through their territory," Cade says.

"Did we cross through their territory?"

Cade nods. "I think so."

"Maybe we shouldn't have done that?"

"Maybe not."

Helpful.

"Even then, they don't usually bother the Unseelie," Revlen says. "The Seelie, on the other hand, they don't much care for."

"Understandably," Esras says. "They hold us accountable for decimating their lands."

Perfect.

"The question is how they knew," Revlen says. "We weren't exactly flying the Seelie flag."

I look over at Esras again. "Do you guys usually ride through centaur territory flying the Seelie flag?"

So far, he's maintaining his dignity pretty well, all things considered. Now, he looks a little embarrassed. "Not me, personally, but yes. That's the tradition. And usually my people only travel outside the city kingdom in large groups."

"Let me guess," I say. "So they can magically kick centaur ass if needed."

"That would be the idea," Esras says. "However, in this case it would seem almost as if they were tipped off."

I look back and forth within our group. "By who?"

"Good question," Revlen says. "Not my people, if that's what you're thinking. I trust them with my life, and have for years."

Actually, I was wondering if it could have been her people. I can only hope she's right.

"I suppose it's possible that they just got lucky," Cade says.

A few moments of silence follow, and then Revlen says, "That is possible."

I can tell she doesn't believe that, but right now I'm not sure how much it matters. How we got into this isn't important, it's how to get out of it again. On top of that, I need to pee.

Which doesn't happen soon. Or at all, as we continue riding for what feels like a lifetime. In truth, it's probably less than an hour. But tell that to a girl with a full bladder tied to a horse. Meanwhile, the centaurs never once speak to us, while occasionally issuing commands to our horses, who obey. Traitors. Andor and I are going to have a serious talk later.

Finally, we arrive at a stretch of forest beside a river. Unlike Lanisan, this forest is alive. The trees are a little on the spindly side, but their branches display leaves showing fall colors. We ride along a path until we come to a clearing, at the center of which there's a large stone fire pit. The pit is crossed by a long metal pole, presumably used for cooking. Not exactly comforting, since I have no idea what centaurs eat. All I can do is hope they think of us as people too, because I sure as hell don't want the word "rotisserie" associated with my death.

To add yet another complication to our current dilemma, the centaur camp is, not surprisingly, home to yet more centaurs. At a glance, I'd say there have to be at least thirty more. What does surprise me is that some of them are women. Why that surprises me, I'm not quite sure. After all, making little centaurs without them would be impossible. I guess it's just because I've never seen them pictured before. Like their male counterparts, they wear no clothes, with just their long hair covering their breasts. As they move about, it becomes evident that they're not too worried about it. If the hair covers the boobs, fine. If the boobs are out there, that's fine too. Also like their male counterparts, the female centaurs are seriously buff. These are definitely not chicks who spend their days chatting at the centaur Starbucks or shopping at the centaur mall. One of them glances at me and snickers, presumably because I'm scrawny. Thanks, lady centaur.

Our captors leave us bound, parked as a group, while they gather with their camp buddies. They talk amongst themselves, again in a language I don't understand. I glance over at Cade, who seems to know what I'm thinking.

"So, yeah, the language thing," he says. "That only seems to apply to the other dimension's equivalent of ourselves."

The implication being human equals fae in Faerie. Centaurs are of Faerie, but they're neither human nor fae, strictly speaking.

"Gotcha," I say. I look back and forth within our group again. "Anyone know what they're saying? Other than our horses, I mean."

I'm only half-joking, since I swear our horses take in every word. They stand with their ears swiveled toward the centaurs. Not that I blame them. There is something decidedly horsey about the centaur language, which is full of snorting, nickering and neighing. Kind of cool, but also seriously weird. Sort of like being around a group of teenage girls.

"I understand them," Esras says. "I'm sure Revlen does as well."

Revlen nods, but keeps listening to the centaurs.

Seriously? When were they going to tell me they speak Centaur? Then again, the centaurs barely spoke while we were riding. The feeling I get is that they're not the most talkative crowd.

Finally, the centaur conversation trails off. They look back at us, some of them appearing very annoyed. Two of them, in particular. Yes, one of them is the same centaur woman who snickered at me before. Awesome.

Revlen speaks under her breath. "They sent word about our capture to the clan elder. He's riding this way and should be here by tomorrow."

"Tomorrow?"

"Look at the bright side," Cade says. "At least they intend to keep us alive that long."

Thank you, Mr. Brightside. I'm all about optimism but, as optimism goes, that's pretty lame.

"True," Revlen says. "They also said we stink."

My mouth drops open. "They seriously said that?"

She shrugs. "When was the last time you showered? I know it's been two days for me. On top of that, centaurs have very keen senses." She nods in their direction again. "Two of them have been ordered to take us to bathe."

I look around, desperately hoping I missed seeing the locker room. I really need to pee. "Bathe where?"

"Presumably, the river," Revlen says. "Here they come now."

Two of the centaurs start heading our way. One is male, the other female. They really are built, both of them, bulging with muscle top to bottom. They wear leather belts slung around their waists, holding sheathed hunting knives. They also both wear crossbows strapped to their backs, presumably in case we try to escape. Although, come to think of it, outrunning a centaur doesn't seem likely. No wonder she was snickering. I only have two tiny little legs.

The two centaurs stop, facing us with stern expressions. The male actually has a handsome face, with a square jaw, dark brown eyes and even features. The female isn't exactly ugly either, at least as far as horse-women go. She has long sandy blonde hair and blue eyes. The guy actually speaks to us, which is a first for this experience.

"My name is Ozenor," he says. He gestures toward his female counterpart. "This is Majenic. We will take you to empty your bladders and bowels. Then you may bathe. If you run, we will kill you."

Okay, a bit blunt, but clearly stated. I can't claim I don't get the rules. It also seems a reasonable deal, all things considered. I finally get to pee somewhere and, if I move slowly enough, I should come out of it alive. I wonder if I should ask about toilet paper.

The centaurs come over, both of them withdrawing their knives to cut our ropes. Majenic takes care of me and Revlen, while Ozenor cuts Cade and Esras loose. I hope this is going where I think it's going, since right now I wouldn't mind splitting up according to gender. It's not like I have body issues, but I draw the line at peeing in the woods for an audience.

"You may get down," Majenic says.

She watches intently as we do, with a frown upon her face. The feeling I get is that she finds the idea of us separating from our horses kind of repulsive. Okay, sure. I can get where she's coming from, but I really don't care. Two legs, four legs, we're all good. Just point me in the direction of the freaking latrine.

*

Thankfully, we do split up, with Majenic in charge of me and Revlen. She trots behind us as we take a path through the woods. She allows us a little privacy while we take care of business, although she never does offer toilet paper. I'm not sure how horse-women go about things, but I don't ask. Majenic seems only so approachable. I'm also pretty sure I don't want to know.

When we get to the river, on the other hand, privacy is out of the question. Majenic stays right with us as she guides us along the river bank. Finally, she stops and jerks her head toward the water. "Strip and wash," she says, folding her arms over her chest. She says nothing more as she stares and waits.

I had considered making a go of it fully dressed, but clearly that's not an option. So, I turn away from Revlen and peel off my clothes. I try leaving my bra and panties on, but I make it all of two steps when Majenic gruffly repeats her order. "Strip and wash!"

Okay, okay! Talk about bossy. I guess I'll be adding this one to my Bizarre Experiences Hall of Fame, which is already getting pretty crowded. The time that giant horse-chick ordered me to get naked. Which I do now, making the mistake of sneaking a peek at Revlen just before we submerge ourselves in the water. Geez. Her body is amazing, toned with muscle, and perfectly proportioned from the flare of her hips to the swell of her breasts. Next to her, pale, skinny and soft, I must look like a wet Chihuahua. This experience is doing nothing for my self-confidence.

But I can't deny that the water feels wonderful, with just the right amount of coolness to give me a jolt and make my body tingle, but warm enough that I quickly adjust. I dunk myself again, scrubbing my hands through my hair, rinsing away two days' worth of sweat, dirt and ash. Despite the extremely weird circumstances, bathing naked in a flowing, fresh river feels like heaven.

Suddenly, I catch movement in my peripheral vision. I turn to look downstream just as Cade and Esras wade out into the river. The water covers them from the waist down, as it does us, but I can't quite tear my eyes away from

Esras. His arms and shoulders are ropes of muscle, his chest broad and powerful. His tan skin glistens in the sunlight, as water drips down his torso toward his tapered waist. Once again, I feel that hunger rise up inside me, an instinctive yearning that once again takes me off guard. It's not just that he's handsome, although there's no doubt that he is. It feels more like something deep in my core needs to be with him. It's strange, and seems to make no sense, but it feels almost like I've known him before in some distant past.

My body reacts as a warm breeze caresses my breasts. Obviously, this isn't the time or place for these feelings, but I've been caught by surprise. I can't help but feel what I feel. Then I realize that Esras is staring back. And that, of course, I'm uncovered from the waist up. Amazingly, he never once looks at Revlen. He keeps his gaze focused entirely on me. Even from a distance, I can see in his eyes that he feels the same way.

CHAPTER 13

We walk in silence back toward the centaur camp. Speaking is all but pointless, since Majenic remains close behind us. In the quiet woods, with no sounds loud enough to muffle our words, there's no way we won't be heard. And, of course, the only relevant topic for conversation would be escape.

I keep wondering how we're going to manage that. We're no longer bound, at least for the moment, so that part is good. On the other hand, the centaurs have taken our horses and weapons, we possess no magic, and we're greatly outnumbered. Add to that, Ozenor's words keep playing in my head. *If you run, we will kill you.* Yep, that part seemed clear, and I'm assuming it applies across the board. All in all, not a great situation.

We get back to see that the camp has changed. Set about twenty yards apart, there are now two large cages. At first, I think they must have been brought from somewhere, but then I realize they've been constructed from the trees themselves. Actual living trees, that have been transformed. Their branches are now inverted and pointing down, woven together and interlocking to leave only gaps a few inches wide between them. Between the blocking wards and now this, it seems clear that the centaurs possess significant magic, powers that clearly don't play by the Seelie rules. If their magic is in any way compromised, I sure as hell wouldn't want to face them when they're in full control.

I keep looking for an angle, thinking there must be a way out, but things just keep getting worse. I have no doubt who those cages are meant for, and soon Revlen and I are marched into one, the interlocked branches creating an opening for just long enough to let us through. Esras and Cade are taken to the other. Again, it's a moment when every fiber of my being wants to resist and fight back. I'm sure the others feel the same way, but in this scenario compliance means continued survival, and so far our lives are not in danger. In fact, other than being captured to begin with, we've suffered no abuse. The treatment has been humane, even approaching considerate of our well-being, although one could argue that the centaurs allowed us to bathe for their own benefit. After all, they couldn't stand the smell of us.

Even now, we're brought a meal of sorts, cups of water and wooden bowls containing berries, other fruits I don't recognize, and strips of what at first I think must be smoked meat. It's not. Apparently, it's some sort of sweet, chewy plant. Revlen and I eat sitting across from each other on the ground.

"I haven't had netchkor in a long time," she says, seeming to savor her portion.

"You've eaten this stuff before?"

"Sure. It's considered a delicacy, although we never quite seem to get it right. The centaurs are naturals when it comes to vegetarian cooking."

A sense of relief ripples through me, as I think of the giant cooking spits I noticed before. "The centaurs are vegetarians?"

"Most of the time," Revlen says.

Okay, great. I should have left well enough alone, and I decide not to pursue it further. Maybe I'm better off not knowing.

Now that no centaur is looming within earshot, it seems safe to talk about our plan. "So, what are we going to do?"

Revlen shrugs, a gesture that doesn't seem quite her natural mode. "Get some rest, I guess. I wasn't exactly ready to get up this morning."

"I meant…" Rather than say it aloud, I gesture with my head to indicate the cage surrounding us.

Revlen finishes chewing one of the berries. "Not sure what we can do other than wait for the clan elder. At which point, we can argue our case." She eats another berry, and then confirms what I was thinking before. "There's no way we could outrun them, even if we managed to escape. Even with our horses, it would be all but impossible."

I try the netchkor again. It's actually not bad. It tastes a little like bacon, but mixed with the tastes of maple and honey. "What do you think our odds are?"

"If it was just me and Cade, I'd say not too bad. I'm not sure what they'd make of you, to be honest. Either way, having Esras with us definitely presents a problem."

There seems no point in again discussing how the centaurs might have known. Obviously, that part remains a mystery. I try again. "So, like, odds?"

Revlen thinks for a moment, and then waggles her hand. "I guess fifty-fifty. It could go either way."

She seems pretty relaxed about it, which I suppose might be a good sign. Then again, Revlen is used to facing danger. In her line of work, that must come with the territory.

"And if it goes bad, do they put us in prison or something?"

Revlen shakes her head. "Centaurs don't have prisons."

Oh.

Revlen stretches out on the ground, elbows out, and with her hands behind her head. "It looks like it's going to be a long day," she says. "If I were you, I'd get some sleep."

With that, she checks out, leaving me still chewing on centaur bacon in a tree cage. I think about asking Majenic for a toothbrush, but decide against it. Instead, I just drink my cup of water and then stretch out on the ground. With any luck, I won't wake up being tossed through the air.

*

That I actually do catch some sleep surprises me. But then, who the hell knows what time it was when I was plucked from my dreams and roped to a horse? On top of that, I was completely worn out by travel the day before. By the time I wake up, the sun is already starting to set.

Revlen sits with her back pressed against the bars of our shared cage. Never one to pull punches, she says, "Did you know you snore?"

Thanks for that. Best road trip ever.

I'm barely done stretching when Majenic shows up again. Apparently, she's been put in charge of our bathroom breaks, which makes me wonder if she's working off demerits or something. Or maybe she's the only woman centaur who can handle being around the stinky creatures who walk on two legs.

After a brief excursion into the woods, we're deposited back into our cage and fed again, basically the same meal we had before. At least Revlen is getting her share of netchkor. Day has turned to night, and it's just me and Revlen enjoying more quality time together again. Still, I figure I might as well take this opportunity to see what makes her tick. After all, the possibility exists that she'll be the last person I ever talk to.

I try to start with something that seems like a safe question. Nothing overly personal. "So, how long have you been with the rebel movement?"

"Since I was ten," she says.

My eyes widen. No, I wasn't exactly ready for that one. "Ten?"

Revlen nods, toying with a sprig she tore off of a branch behind her. I'm not sure it's a good idea to piss off the tree cage, but I don't say anything.

"That's when the Seelie killed my brother. That's when *Vintain* killed him, to be specific."

So much for sticking to impersonal questions, but my eyes rivet upon her as my heart starts to beat faster. "Vintain killed your brother? I'm sorry."

Revlen absently bends the sprig into a loop. "The queen came through town with her entourage, and my brother refused to kneel."

The food in my stomach turns to lead. "That was all he did?"

Revlen pulls on the loop, tying it into a knot. "That's all he did. If the queen rides past, you're supposed to kneel. My brother thought it was wrong to expect that from us. He felt that the Unseelie weren't her people. That she cared nothing about our kind, and that she only made our lives miserable. So, yes, he refused. And Vintain struck him down."

I narrow my eyes as my vision starts to telescope with hate. "That bastard." When I thought I couldn't hate Vintain any more, I feel my loathing suddenly triple.

Revlen turns her amber eye on me, her face set like stone, leaving no doubt that she feels exactly the same way. "It was just me and Tamor that day. We were walking home from the market. I was just a girl, and he was a teenager. I don't know, maybe he felt a real sense of conviction. Or maybe he was just showing off. Either way, he didn't think he'd be killed for it. Yelled at, maybe. Pushed around, possibly. But killed? No."

I stare at the ground, my vision blurring even more as I fight back tears. I can't allow myself to break down. Not now. I need to know as much as possible. I force myself to meet Revlen's gaze again.

Revlen starts winding another knot in the sprig. "That's when this happened," she says. She taps her eye patch. "Little ten year old me tried to retaliate. My efforts were met with the tip of Vintain's blade."

This time, my stomach twists with both rage and horror. I speak softly. "I'm so sorry I asked. I shouldn't have."

Revlen shakes her head. "No, it's fine. Everyone else knows my story. Why shouldn't you? You're one of us now."

In that moment, I realize she's right. If I had any doubts about that before, I no longer do. Her cause is now my cause, and if we don't die here, I'll die by her side to see it through. Revlen is right, we all have stakes in this game. And mine, as much as they mean to me, are no more important than hers.

"Thank you," I say.

Revlen nods, as if she's known all along that I'd reach this point. But, then again, in her experience those around her must eventually all realize they're in it together.

"I recovered well enough," she says. "Physically, that is. Psychologically, everything changed that day. In my heart, I became a rebel, and I knew nothing would ever change that back again. Nothing ever will. I'll keep fighting until things change, or until I die trying."

That part, I already sensed in her. Everything about her speaks of resolve and commitment. "What about Esras? How long has he been involved?"

"Since he was seventeen," Revlen says. "That was when he brought us some half-blood strays. He captured them after they'd wandered into Seelie territory. They feared the worst, of course, but Esras took them for their own good. He delivered them to us and we got them out again. If he'd been caught, he would have been executed, his family disgraced. That didn't stop him. He's been working with us since."

When I wondered before about how much Esras was willing to risk, I now have the answer. He's remained willing to risk everything.

"And Cade?" I say.

Revlen smiles fondly. Apparently, she finds Cade cute too. "We got word of Cade's special skills. So, we enlisted him to procure a few items helpful to the cause. And, of course, it's a good idea to occasionally remind the Seelie that they're not impervious. Breaching their security measures, and wandering through their homes, is a good way of delivering that message."

"I get the feeling that, these days, that's primarily why Cade steals," I say. "Well, that and to pay for beer in Silvermist."

Revlen laughs. "Cade has personal reasons for being involved, of course. But, often, it's those personal reasons that make for the strongest commitment."

It's the same for all three of them, I realize. For Revlen, what happened to her brother. For Esras, his sister. And for Cade, his future with the woman he loves. Their commitment might be ideologically driven, but it's grounded in personal loss.

"What about the other half-bloods? They seem a little on the fence."

Revlen ties another knot in her sprig. "Definitely mixed opinions, from what we hear. Some hate the Seelie. Others, believe it or not, are actually proud of their Seelie heritage. Despite how it came about, they view it as something linking them to royalty. Of course, there are others who just—"

Revlen stops at the sound of hoofbeats pounding the earth. We go to the front of our cage and peer out, as a group of centaurs gallops past. They're heading away from camp. In the distance, we see what looks like the light of torches approaching.

"If I was to guess," Revlen says. "I'd say that the clan elder may have arrived earlier than expected."

CHAPTER 14

They leave us waiting until they feel good and ready. Maybe it's an hour, but it might as well be a week, as we wait to face our judgement. As Majenic appears, uttering a centaur incantation to part the living bars of our cage, Revlen mutters, "At least they didn't make us wait all night."

She definitely has a point. There's no way we would have managed to get more sleep anyway, and spending the night anticipating this moment would have been torture.

The camp, left dark before, is now alight with torches. They blaze in rows lining the path we walk as a group, the four of us together again. We're taken to where the torches ring their way around a cleared out cul-de-sac. Within that circle, the centaurs stand gathered facing the one who must be their elder. We're taken to the front to face him too.

He doesn't appear half as old as I imagined. Although his face is creased, and his hair and beard both gray, his arms and chest bulge with muscle. The bronze skin of his upper body glistens as he stands before a fire burning between him and us.

"I am Rontauk," he says, regarding us with a fierce gaze. "My people received a bird warning them of your imminent crossing through our land."

Bird? Did I hear that right?

Seeing my expression, Cade whispers, "Lingualawk. Messenger bird."

I imagine something like a carrier pigeon, but that notion is soon dispelled.

"The bird specified that he'd flown in over your party," Rontauk says. "He confirmed that there was indeed a Seelie noble traveling with you."

Okay, yeah. That's a pretty advanced bird. Definitely a Faerie thing.

Rontauk turns to Revlen, possibly because he recognizes her as being Unseelie. Or, because she's super hot. It's impossible to say, but for some reason he singles her out as being the voice for our group. "How can you explain this?"

Revlen swallows, but keeps her gaze fixed on Rontauk. "The Seelie noble is aiding our cause against the crown. We're travelling together to Longmeadow."

Rontauk's face remains rigid. "Why?"

Revlen hesitates, but then gestures toward me. "We seek safe haven for this woman."

Rontauk's eyes barely flick my way before he addresses Revlen again. "Why?"

Revlen considers for a couple of moments. "She has abilities we hope to use against the Seelie. They've learned of her presence."

Rontauk shifts his gaze to me again, studying me more closely this time. "She's a half-blood. Why doesn't she return to her own realm?"

Revlen doesn't argue Rontauk's determination that I'm a half-blood. Which I guess makes sense. Why open that door? "She chose not to. She's working with us and her commitment to the cause compels her to stay."

Rontauk nods. "I see."

He looks past her, and just barely nods toward someone behind us. Ozenor trots forward to meet him. They speak in whispers, using their own language for a couple of minutes. I watch their expressions and gestures, which remain relaxed. The conversation seems casual, not particularly charged. Hopefully, Revlen spelled things out well enough and we'll be okay.

Finally, Ozenor nods and trots back to where he stood before. This time Rontauk fixes his gaze on Esras. "We find it difficult to believe that a Seelie noble such as yourself would protect a half-blood, regardless of her supposed abilities. We also find it difficult to believe that you would work against your own people. Not one of you has for hundreds of years, even as our lands have continued to wither. Can you prove you are, indeed, working for the Unseelie cause?"

It's an impossible request. How can Esras possibly prove such a thing? Amazingly, he retains his composure. He keeps his gaze fixed on Rontauk. "I can offer no proof," he says. "We can only offer our word."

Rontauk nods, but the stillness of his expression makes my stomach sink. It's one of those moments when I just know. I'm soon proven correct.

"Then we find your group guilty of altering nature. Your execution will be carried out after the ceremony of ghosts."

Rontauk says nothing more. Immediately, hands clamp around my upper arms. One of the centaurs behind me holds me in a vise-like grip. I struggle, but it's no use. I desperately look around, my head whipping back and forth, but it's the same for the rest of us. Even Esras's physical strength is no match. This time, our captors don't let go of any one of us as we're delivered back to our cages.

CHAPTER 15

Revlen sits with her legs crossed and her eye closed as the minutes pass. She's remained this way since we've been isolated again. Her breathing, rapid at first, now rises and falls evenly as she appears to have reached a point of inner calm. I'm not sure what she's doing, but I also feel sure I should wait to speak. Eventually, she takes one long deep breath, and then opens her eye again.

"Are you okay?" she says.

She delivers the question so calmly that I'm not sure how to react. That she appears so relaxed, after what we've just been told, reminds me once more that I'm not in my realm. I'm nowhere near it. I start pacing back and forth again, as I've been doing since she went into some sort of meditative coma. "No, I'm not okay! Are you freaking serious?"

Again, Revlen speaks softly. "I'm sorry. I thought you'd be making peace. We don't have much time left."

"Wait, you're a rebel leader. Aren't you going to fight?"

Revlen cocks her head. "How?"

It's a great question. It's also one for which I have no answer. "I don't know. Shit!"

Again, Revlen nods. "I understand your fear and frustration. Our situation appears to be hopeless."

Yeah, we're on the same page now for sure. Before I voice that thought, Revlen continues. "I'll die knowing my fellow rebels will continue the cause. I've sent my thoughts their way, to let them know I'll be leaving."

"Wait. Can they hear you?"

"Maybe not consciously, but we believe we're all connected. They'll feel my departure on a deeper level."

Okay, perfect. Just what I was hoping to hear, that the fae have a woo-woo side. Which doesn't seem all that important right now. So I finally get to ask the question that's been on my mind. "What's the ceremony of ghosts?"

"A centaur ritual for those about to be executed," Revlen says. "They call upon the spirits of their ancestors to guide the newly freed souls into the afterlife."

I shake my head briskly, trying to make sense of that. "*Their* ancestors! What about our ancestors?"

Revlen quirks an eyebrow, which I suspect is usually her version of shrugging. "They don't know our ancestors. How could they call on them?"

The logic in this place kills me. I pace back and forth a few more times. "Let me be sure I've got this right. They kill us, but then call out the welcome wagon."

"Opposite order, really, but that's the general idea. It's a unique tradition."

"Yeah, I'd be really touched if I wasn't going to die soon." I don't mention the veil witch temporary immortality thing for a couple of reasons. First, because no one seems to know the shelf-life of that particular supernatural perk. It's like we're kept in the game until we're not needed anymore. Then, well, apparently we're not needed anymore. The other reason—and this is the one really freaking me out—is that I have no idea if it even applies if I'm in a different realm.

"I'm hardly an expert on centaur rituals," Revlen says, "but I'd imagine they're fine with us calling on our own spiritual ancestors. All I know is that the ceremony is intended for our comfort. As we mentioned before, the centaurs aren't a cruel people. Before the magical blight, they rarely resorted to violence of any kind."

"But now they kill you for trespassing. That's quite the shift in policy."

Revlen considers that for a moment. "Well, to be fair, the Seelie practices did devastate their lands. And we were traveling with a Seelie noble."

I see her point, but she also seems overly centered for a time like this. I start pacing again. "But we're going to make a break for it, right? We're not going down without a fight, are we?"

Revlen studies me calmly again. "If an opportunity presents itself, we'll definitely act. I assure you."

"Okay, good." Damn, for a minute there I thought she was giving up.

"But I highly doubt there'll be an opportunity. The centaurs are known to be very organized and highly observant. So, it might be best to make your peace while there's still time."

Apparently, Revlen decides this conversation has gotten us as far as it's going to go. She closes her eye again, and then goes back to that even breathing thing. Meanwhile, I go back to pacing. Maybe it's part of being a rebel warrior that allows her to remain this calm in the face of death. And, I suppose, in a way it might even be admirable. But I don't have a team of trained insurgents who are going to carry out my cause. If I don't rescue Julia, she doesn't get rescued.

*

I'm still pacing, my heart pounding a million miles a minute, when suddenly a drum starts beating. Once, twice, a third time. And it keeps on beating in that same steady rhythm. Shit. This can't be good.

"I guess it's time," Revlen says.

I feel like screaming, *"How the fuck can you stay this calm!?"* But I don't. It won't do any good, and I don't want being totally freaked out to be my final act. Then again, I'm totally freaking out.

Hooves rapidly approach, the magical cage door parts, and four centaurs enter. All of them are male this time. Maybe Majenic grew fond of us, or maybe she's only working prisoner potty breaks this month, but in the time it takes me to get in a couple of desperate swings I find myself pinned. Soon my wrists are bound behind my back. It's the same for Revlen, who didn't waste her time making a fool of herself by putting up a pointless struggle. Okay, yeah, I get it. She's a realist. We're in the middle of nowhere, unarmed, without magic, and surrounded by centaurs. We're not going anywhere unless they want us to.

We're marched outside as the drum keeps beating. Well, Revlen is marched, while I'm lifted off the ground and carried since I refuse to move my feet. No, I'm not a realist, and it looks like I'm going out that way.

Then I see Esras and Cade, both bound as well, but also upholding their dignity by refusing to carry on. Cade does look frightened, and I can tell he's trying to keep it together. Esras walks with his back straight and his head held high. Nothing in his bearing signals that he's guilty of anything other than being of noble birth. I know him well enough now to understand that he's carried the guilt of his privileged status for his entire life. His eyes meet mine and, within them, I see a gentle regret. I know instinctively that it's regret for us not having had more time together.

And it really starts to sink in that this is it. I'm going to die. No surprise rebel platoon is going to suddenly swoop in and save us. My magic isn't going to kick in and allow me to open a rift for us to run through. And all I can think about is just how pissed off Autumn is going to be at me. I stop struggling. Screw it. I might as well try to maintain some self-respect.

We're led back down the torch-lit path and into the cul-de-sac, where the solemn faces of gathered centaurs stare back at us. They don't look the least bit happy about killing us. If anything, they seem almost sad. But I guess they figure they can't mess around when it comes to dealing with those who wrecked their world. In a moment of completely unexpected empathy, I find myself almost feeling bad for them. That moment passes quickly when I see four nooses hanging from the trees. I so totally don't want to go out that way. I wonder if we might work out a deal. Maybe I flick flies off their hides in exchange for a quick and painless death. I don't know. Something.

Rontauk is the last one to come down the path, emerging from the darkness and into the flickering torchlight. He takes his place again on the other side of the fire, facing us and those surrounding us. "We will begin the ceremony of ghosts," he says, his baritone voice ringing out as he spreads his arms to the night.

Rontauk closes his eyes and begins softly reciting a string of words. He speaks in the centaur language, maintaining a steady murmur. I have no idea if it might be an incantation or a prayer. The drumbeat continues, and I realize that this time it's meant to summon the dead.

My eyes widen as suddenly a blast of sparks rises from the fire, spiraling into the night. The fire surges upward as smoke plumes swirl, and then settles back down. I'm almost convinced that all of this is just for show, but that's when I see them.

They come trotting out of the forest, a line of centaur spirits. At first they flicker as they approach, like so many of the ghosts I've seen before not yet fully manifesting in this plane. They continue to grow less translucent, more solid, as Rontauk continues his chant.

I look back and forth between Revlen, Cade and Esras. They continue staring straight ahead, their eyes fixed upon the fire. I look past those in my condemned party to see it's the same for the centaurs. Some stare at the flames, and others look around, but not one of them looks in the right direction. The centaurs don't see the ghosts. With one exception.

Rontauk's eyes track their progress as they grow closer, both of us gazing the same way. Suddenly his eyes cut to me, as I alone watch with him. In that moment, I can tell he knows. And, as always happens when I'm in the presence of ghosts, they're drawn to me. They stride past Rontauk and their living brethren, to congregate before me. Some cock their heads in curiosity, while others reach out. I reach out too, brushing my fingers against those extended toward me. The ghosts encircle me, passing through those standing in their way as they canter around me. One by one, each of them starts to reach out, touching my hand as they pass.

Rontauk openly gapes, not even trying to hide the stunned expression that's taken over his face. Soon, all heads turn. The entire camp watches me, not seeing what only I and Rontauk see, but knowing they're experiencing something completely unexpected. The energy suddenly shifts, from that of a group collected to address matters of this world, to one beholding another world making its presence known.

The circling ghosts slow, and then come to a stop. I fix my attention on the one directly before me, a woman. I can't be sure how old she was when she died—she's from an entirely different race of beings—but I'd guess somewhere in her middle age. She has light blue eyes and graying blonde hair.

The words just come to me, as they always do in my role as a veil witch. "I can help you," I say. "If you'd like to leave this plane, I can help you leave."

She studies me with wondering eyes, then suddenly steps back. Her mouth drops open, as before me a glowing white orb appears. Even in this realm, with my hands bound, this one intrinsic magic comes to me. As I knew it would. I don't have to look around to know that all gathered here see it too. I can feel their collected confusion and astonishment.

The ghost centaur raises her eyes to mine again. Her lips don't move, but I hear her speak. *We have sworn an oath. We must stay with our people during this time.*

I nod my understanding, and the orb floating before me fades, then winks out. I hear those around me draw in a collective breath.

The ghost nods to me one more time, and then suddenly turns away. She goes to where Rontauk stands, as the other ghosts follow. They gather as a group, listening as the one who spoke to me now addresses the clan elder. Suddenly, he raises his arm and the drumming stops. The ghosts begin to fade, becoming translucent again, then flickering until they no longer remain.

Rontauk's voice rises into the night, as he points to me. "Our ancestors have spoken. The afterworld will not hold this one. She's needed here. Cut their bonds and set them free."

CHAPTER 16

The sun is still rising as we ride through the prairie, and I'm told that we should soon reach Dabria's village. Since leaving the centaur camp in the middle of the night, we've encountered no other signs of human life. Well, fae life. Not that I'm complaining. Less than twelve hours ago, I felt sure we were about to die, and I'll breathe a heavy sigh of relief when we get to where we're going. I realize it was unsafe for me to stay in Scintillia, but things haven't exactly gone smoothly since leaving.

I keep scanning the prairie while seeing nothing. Each time we crest a hill, I see only more miles of prairie before me. I really hope these guys know where they're going. If they're wrong, what's next? A band of hostile gnomes?

Finally, Esras says, "There, look."

He points to the distance, and at first I don't see anything. But then a flicker of motion catches my eye. I see a small, thin figure running away. I imagine it to be a young boy, but I can't be sure. He's too far away and quickly gone again, disappearing behind a swell of tall grass waving in the breeze.

"Sentry?" Cade says.

"Could be," Revlen says. "Or just someone out trapping, but it doesn't matter. They'll soon know we're here."

I look back and forth between them. "But that's okay, right? Are we talking about the people who live where we're going?"

Esras nods. "We were hoping to send Cade ahead, once we got a little closer."

"Why?"

Cade answers my question. "People out here have to be careful. Don't worry. We'll be fine."

Seriously, don't worry? I really need to let Cade know how I feel about that phrase.

Soon, Revlen's prediction proves true as we see dust rising in the distance. Not long after, hooves pound the earth as a group of riders becomes visible on the horizon. We slow our approach and wait.

There turn out to be four of them, all men and all armed with swords. Two of them have bows strapped to their backs, along with quivers of arrows. Those two hold back, while the other two approach. I get the idea. If something bad goes down, the archers can pick us off from a distance.

As they ride closer, the two figures grow more distinct. One man is older, perhaps middle-aged, his tan face lined and his hair streaked with gray. The other looks to be about our age, maybe a little younger. Otherwise, they share a resemblance, both strongly muscled, with bright blue eyes, square jaws and broad noses. I can only guess that they must be father and son. I brace myself for the worst, but both men squint at Cade as smiles spread across their faces.

The younger man speaks first. "Scamper, good to see you!"

Oh, my God. Scamper. There it is again. I really need to start using that.

"You as well, Jodelac," Cade calls back. "Sent you out to greet us, did they?"

The older one speaks next. "We got word you were coming. How are you, son?"

That one gets a double-take from me, but clearly they were somehow informed that we were coming.

"I'm fine," Cade says. "It's good to see you, Gylth. How's Dabria?"

Of course, Gylth must be Dabria's father, Jodelac presumably her brother.

Suddenly, Gylth stops in his tracks. He holds his arm out to keep his son from riding forward. His eyes narrow as he takes in Esras.

"It's okay," Cade says. "He's with the cause."

I guess seeing Cade first, and then Esras, was enough to process. But now Gylth becomes aware of Revlen. "Is it true?"

She nods. "Yes. Esras is with us."

Gylth lowers the arm meant to protect his son. "If you say so, of course." The smile returns to his face. "Well, then. Let's get where we're going."

We ride forward, as Gylth and Jodelac fall in beside us. Soon, the archers do the same, although they too appear stunned at seeing Esras. And I guess it makes sense that Revlen didn't send word about him being with us ahead of our arrival. Obviously, it's not a secret you'd want to get out. Although, come to think of it, the centaurs pulled that off with one of their lingualawks. Those horse people really are on top of their game.

Cade turns to Gylth again. "Wait, when I said Esras was with the cause, you hesitated. When Revlen said it, you believed her."

Gylth laughs. "Exactly. You never change, Scamper, do you?"

What that means, I'm not sure, but Cade shoots me a look that pretty much says it all. I get it. His would be future father-in-law has a hard time taking him seriously. Oh, Scamper, my nerdy thieving buddy. Can you blame him?

We ride for another mile or so, and finally the town becomes visible. When it does, I realize why I had such a hard time spotting it before. Compared to anything I'm used to, it's tiny. From our approach, it appears to be little more than a cluster of buildings, twenty or thirty at the most, out on a vast prairie and nestled beside a river and a copse of trees. The buildings also blend in perfectly with their surroundings, and it isn't until we're actually upon them that I can make out roofs thatched with prairie grass, and walls of reddish brown clay. Clearly, this little outpost was designed to be invisible.

Soon, we ride through what reminds me of a medieval village. The buildings are nearly identical, each simple and small. I assume most to be dwellings, while a few at the center of the town, somewhat larger, might be for meetings, storage or possibly commerce. People crane to look at us, some seeming mildly curious, others openly staring. The feeling I get is that those living here don't see many outsiders. There's no doubt that Esras is the main object of their curiosity. It seems clear that he's recognized as being at least a Seelie, if not a noble. Thankfully, we're with Gylth and Jodelac, the other riders having gone on their way. These two familiar faces serve to set minds at ease.

Before long, we reach Gylth's house at the far end of the village. It's identical to the others we passed, little more than a cottage with a garden beside it and a well. Inside, I wonder if we'll find only one shared space, but walls divide the house into rooms. Although, none reach the pitched ceiling. At one end, a ladder ascends to a loft, spanning half the house.

A woman who must be Gylth's wife stands inside waiting to greet us. Like her husband, she appears in some ways middle-aged, her face lightly creased and her hair showing traces of gray. But she too looks strong and fit, her figure showing not an ounce of fat. She wears a simple beige dress, revealing legs and arms that are tanned and toned.

"I'm Tayora," she says. "Welcome. We're pleased to have you."

As we introduce ourselves, she nervously spins a ring on her finger. A little strain shows in her face as well. I'm not sure what's at the root of it. Could it be fear at the risk they're taking? That has to weigh on her, at least a little. For that matter, the whole village would be at risk if the Seelie found out. I can only guess that our coming must have been discussed.

Tayora gestures toward a doorway. "You must be hungry and thirsty. Please, make yourselves comfortable."

I can't help but notice that, so far, she addresses Cade no differently than us. I suppose his presence as part of the rebel cause might be new to her. The way she keeps twisting that ring suggests it's the case.

We enter the kitchen, where a young woman works at the stove. She turns as we enter, and she's exactly as Cade described. Dabria has thick brown hair falling in curls to her shoulders. She has big brown eyes, a rosebud mouth and a smattering of freckles. And, of course, slender ears rising to points. Her eyes sweep over us to land on Cade, and they take each other in. Each has a smile tugging at their lips. In a silent moment, so much passes between them. Longing. Love. Joy at seeing each other. And just a tinge of palpable sadness. I've seen people who communicate less in three weeks than these two do in three silent seconds.

Tayora breaks the spell. "Dabria, are the dupple rings ready?"

Cade's face lights up. "You made dupple rings?"

His reaction is boyish and natural, his enthusiasm speaking to his comfort here. Under different circumstances, I bet he's like part of the family. Although, if anyone else made the dupple rings—whatever they are—I doubt he'd be half as excited.

Dabria smiles more openly this time. Her eyes linger on Cade's. Then she remembers that it was her mother who asked the first question. "Yes, they're almost ready," she says. Her eyes travel to Cade again, before she turns back to the stove.

Tayora gestures to where plates have been laid out, upon a simple table constructed from planks. "Please, have a seat," she says. "I'm afraid you'll have to pardon the poor state of our table. It sometimes doubles as my husband's workbench."

Her eyes cut briefly to Esras as she says it, betraying the true source of her nervousness. Suddenly, I make the connection. She's self-conscious at having a noble in her home. Despite everything, some part of her remains trained to view them as being superior.

Esras's cheeks color at her words. It's an awkward moment, which he saves by saying, "I can think of no greater honor. Thank you for offering."

Jodelac cracks a smile. "If we're done with the formalities, can we please eat?"

"Good idea," Gylth says. "Have a seat, everyone. I'll get the tea. Sorry, but there's no coffee out here. One of the few things I miss about the city, actually."

Jodelac starts to sit and his mother says, "Not so fast, mister. Get the muffins and honey first."

Now it's Jodelac whose cheeks grow red, but he does as he's been told.

We take seats at the table, as Gylth brings tea and Jodelac the muffins and honey. Tayora lays out plates of cheese and bowls of fruit. Dabria joins us last, bringing her platter of dupple rings, setting one upon each of our plates before she sits down. Cade isn't the only one, I notice, eagerly eyeing what look like flat donuts glistening with glaze and sprinkled with confectioner's sugar.

Cade looks at me across the table, a grin tugging at the corner of his mouth. "You like dupple rings, right Cassie?"

I hesitate, not wanting to blow my cover.

Gylth is the first to laugh, but then the others join in. I look around, confused.

"We know where you're from," Gylth says. "It's okay. Revlen told us. Go on and try your dupple ring."

Now it's my turn to blush, as everyone stares.

"Go on," Cade says.

Thanks, Cade.

I slice my fork through the glazed batter, which parts to reveal a bright purple center. Weird. Since everyone keeps staring, I slice again and raise that small wedge to my mouth. My eyes pop wide as a blend of succulent fruit and warm sugary dough melts against my taste buds. Everyone bursts out laughing at the stunned expression I can't manage to hide.

"Now you get it," Cade says.

"Cade told us you don't have dupples in your realm," Dabria says.

"Nope, definitely no dupples," I say, as I dig in for more.

"I may miss city coffee," Gylth says, "but I'll trade it for country dupples any day. They don't grow any better than they do right here."

Thankfully, everyone turns their attention to their own dupple rings, leaving me to my private ecstasy. I try not to eyeball the platter, but it looks like there are enough for us to each have one more. Phew.

"So, here's what we're thinking." Gylth gestures to indicate me and Revlen. "You two will share the loft with Dabria." He turns to Esras and Cade. "You two will share a room with Jodelac. How does that sound?"

His point seems clear. Maybe this is really about Dabria and Cade, but we better not get any ideas. This is an old-fashioned Unseelie house and the same rule applies across the board. There'll be no hanky panky under this roof.

"Absolutely," Revlen says. "We hope not to inconvenience you for long."

Tayora shakes her head. "It's no inconvenience. We're happy to help."

"Speaking of which," Gylth says. "What's going on in Scintillia? Reliable word seldom makes it this far."

"The city appears to be destabilizing rapidly," Revlen says. "Which is both good and bad. On one hand, it means we can likely take action soon. On the other hand, the Seelie know they're losing control. They keep resorting to desperate measures."

Tayora's eyes cut quickly to, and away from, Esras. It happens fast, but doesn't go unnoticed by him.

"It's okay," he says, and then he waits for Tayora to meet his gaze. "I realize what my people have done. And I'm sorry that the actions of the few, over such a long time, reflect poorly on so many. But I'm more sorry for the indignities your people have suffered. I assure you, that in coming here, I've chosen a side. So, please speak freely."

After a moment, Tayora nods. "Thank you."

Dabria leans in toward us, but directs her question to Cade. "What about Silvermist?"

"Not good," he says. "People are split, but at least some seem to be galvanizing."

"Maybe they can help," Dabria says. "After all, what's going on here affects them too."

"Absolutely," Revlen says. "But we can't count on it. We may not have that kind of time. I strongly suspect we don't."

Gylth turns his attention to me. "Revlen's message was brief, but she said you came to rescue a friend. Is your friend from Silvermist?"

If he knows where I'm from, I don't understand why he seems to make this assumption. Although, I do plan on helping Helen, Lily and Mitch too.

"No, she's from my realm," I say.

My words are met with a moment of silence. Then, Tayora says, "But that would mean…"

"Yes, a changeling," Revlen says.

Tayora doesn't say anything, but behind her eyes I see the wheels turning.

But it's Dabria who goes where her mother fears to tread. "I thought changeling spells couldn't be broken," she says "I mean, it's never happened."

"But it has," Esras says. He looks at me, his meaning clear.

Gylth all but slams down his mug of tea, his eyes going wide. A grin spreads across his face. "You broke a changeling spell?"

"Yes," I say. And it's not so much a feeling of pride that swells up within me, as the sudden realization that I too can give them hope.

Gylth shakes his head, as if to make sure he heard right. "Are you sure?"

"Father," Dabria says. "Obviously, she'd know."

Gylth gives his daughter a mock-scowl, and then turns to me again. "Well, damn," he says. "Someone get this woman another dupple ring."

CHAPTER 17

Other than the night when we rode out of the city, the next two days are the only time I've known in Faerie when I didn't feel threatened, trapped or as if I was about to die. We help out Dabria's family, working with them in their gardens and tending to their animals. We visit their orchard to collect fruit. Yes, I see my very first dupple tree, resisting the urge to fall to my knees in praise. We mill the fae version of corn for flour. We help fix a fence, and start a new well. Gylth and Tayora keep insisting we don't need to work, that they're more than happy to have us as guests. Still, we assure them that we're happy to help. Which is true.

During these times, I watch Esras. I haven't known him long, but it's the first time he hasn't had a pained look in his eye, or a muscle working at his jaw. He relaxes and smiles, jokes and laughs. He works hard when given the chance, never once expecting thanks or credit. I can tell I'm seeing him as he truly is, a man with no interest in riches, status or influence. A man who only wants peace, both within himself and for those around him—a peace he's dreamed of since his sister died.

We also rest as much as possible. For me, that's not easy to do. Each day spent is another knowing that Julia remains held captive. As well as the others from my realm, those teenagers taken along with who can say how many more. I've wondered about them too, of course, many times. If I fail Julia, do I fail them all? From what I know, I can only assume that the answer is yes. And how could I ever begin to know where they all went, to even try bringing them back?

The fact is, I just don't know. All I can do is learn a little at a time, while waiting for the next opportunity to make things change. I try telling myself that's enough for now. That it's all I can do. That I need to trust in those around me to keep leading me forward. And, that, right now, I should rest while I can.

On the third night after dinner, we gather behind Dabria's house, where her father lights a fire in a small pit. We share a bottle of wine, and then another. Above us, the stars shine and a mild breeze blows through my hair. The flames flicker and dance. Those around me talk of other times, perhaps not entirely good, but not as bad as the ones they now face. I learn more about their realm, about their beliefs, their customs and history. For that brief time, as the wine warms my stomach and the fire my skin, I finally feel like a welcome visitor in this place called Faerie.

At one point, Gylth says, "Tell us about your realm, Cassie. We know so little about it."

Good lord, where to begin? I think for a few moments, and then tell them about countries, politics, and war. About races, strife and progress. I describe computers, cell phones and the internet. Before I know it, I find myself rambling on, but no one seems bored. Just the opposite, as they raptly listen. At one point, they ask about music and it gets ridiculous with them asking me to sing. I actually do, because I've had enough wine. We all laugh as I both try and fail to reach a high note in my solo rendition of Bohemian Rhapsody. "Scaramouche, Scaramouche, will you do the fandango?"

"What's a fandango?" Tayora asks.

I admit that I have no idea, and we all laugh that much harder.

Later, Gylth and Tayora beg off, saying they're tired. Not long after, Revlen claims the same, although I suspect she's hoping to avoid being a fifth wheel. Of course, you'd have to be blind not to notice the attraction Cade and Dabria share. At the same time, I feel sure Revlen noticed that moment between Esras and me that day at the river. It's difficult not to observe what passes between four naked people suddenly encountering each other.

We sit for a while more, but I'm not surprised when Esras says, "I was thinking I might take a walk. Anyone interested?"

"Sure," I say.

And, of course, Cade and Dabria decide they're fine where they are. Which was at least half the point to begin with, allowing the two of them some time alone. So far, they appear to have had none. Although, my pulse picks up a little, since I get the feeling that Esras wouldn't mind being alone with me.

Soon, we walk through the quiet streets of the village. It doesn't seem very late, maybe ten or eleven, but most of the houses around us are dark. Which I guess makes sense, given that the people here seem more aligned to the rising and setting of the sun than to any sort of clock.

We reach the end of a street and keep walking a path out into the prairie. The only sound comes from a breeze rustling the grass, causing it to undulate like gently rolling surf in the moonlight. Above us, glittering stars are spread out across an inky sky.

"Do you feel it?" Esras says.

Under different circumstances, it would probably be a confusing question, but I know exactly what he means. I've felt it each day, growing stronger since we left the centaur camp. It's the energy of the ley line reaching out, almost as if she's searching, although her power hasn't yet come back to me as it did on the night when I rescued Ellie.

"They've got it locked down again, don't they?" Even from this far away, I can feel it.

Esras nods. "I'm sure you're right, but the magic of this realm is strong. Some say stronger than all others. Some of that energy still manages to escape. In places like this, you can feel it."

I nod toward the village behind us. "Can they feel it?"

"A little, I'm sure."

It's Esras's way of being kind, but the implication is clear. They may feel it, but not like we do. And it's the first time I notice that he never put that ring back on, after the centaurs returned it to him. He may choose to access that power when we return, but I suspect he's broken that last connection with his people.

The moon illuminates Esras's face, enough so that I see the playful smile tugging at his lips. "Maybe you should try it," he says. "You know you want to."

And he's right, I do. I feel the magic rising inside me, making my nerve endings tingle. He's tempting me, knowing I want to be tempted.

"Maybe just a little," I say.

Esras's smile grows. "Exactly. Just to keep in practice. You don't want to get rusty."

He doesn't have to say more. I will the magic into me, and it accepts my invitation. That current surges through me, and even this far from the compromised ley line, I remind myself to be careful. I haven't forgotten what happened the last time I gained access to fae magic. Even as I think it, from somewhere either deep inside, or very far away, I hear a voice say, *Your fae magic.*

I expect to conjure an orb or a fireball, a flare to light up the night. At the last instant I feel a new possibility within me. I raise my hand, thrust it out, and an arc of blue lightning streaks through the air.

I jump back and laugh. "Whoa. What was that?"

Esras speaks softly, sounding a bit stunned. "Fae magic," he confirms.

I try again, thrusting out once more, but this time grabbing hold of one end of the lightning before it arcs away. It shouldn't work, but it still does. The light I grabbed hold of wraps itself around my wrist and I snap it like a whip. A crack sounds at the other end, and a blue flash lights up the night.

"That's suspension magic," Esras says. "If you hit a living thing, it would be immobilized."

Within my mind, I see images of Lauren Flannery suspended in her moment of death. Is the magic I just made related somehow to that which Vintain used? Something tells me yes, that here a mage powerful enough could use magic like this for many purposes.

Esras snaps me out of it, grinning now. "Let's see what else you got."

I can't help but smile back, as those other thoughts fade from my mind. "Was that a challenge?"

"I suppose you could interpret it that way."

"I do."

Esras starts backing away, that smile still on his face. "Then I challenge you to a duel. Magical weapon of your choice."

"Excuse me?"

Esras laughs, and I know I'm seeing a part of him that I couldn't have if we hadn't come here. Within him still lives a carefree young man, poised to play games and compete. "You heard me. Take a shot. It's not like you can hurt me."

I narrow my eyes. "Remember whose idea this was, pal."

Esras laughs again, but then jumps back as I thrust out. A blast of light streaks toward him, this time a swirling green electrical sphere. He thrusts his hand out too, countering with a bright white lightning bolt. My sphere explodes in a shower of sparks, shooting out like fireworks.

I stride toward him. "Really?"

He walks toward me too. "Yeah, really," he says, imitating what, to his ear, must be my accent. "Is that all you've got?"

I have to laugh at his impression of me. "Not even close."

We thrust out our palms once more. Two charges streak through the air to meet and explode. Fireworks shoot out again, cascading around us, as we continue closing the gap between ourselves. We do the same again, our magical energy colliding, this time with a burst of light just before our faces. Each time, I tell myself it's not possible. But, each time, it grows stronger. My body tingles and vibrates as his magic mingles with my own, somehow coursing through my veins.

We stop, facing each other, just a foot apart. My chest rises and falls as I catch my breath. Then he reaches out to take hold of my hand. With just that much, his magic arcs through me. Then he pulls me in and his soft lips part mine. Once again, I'm on fire. I shudder with pleasure as a tingling sensation spreads down the length of my stomach. Our breath mingles, wet and warm, our tongues wrapping around each other in a sensual dance. Heat keeps building at my core, rippling through me stronger and stronger, to the point where I can't help panting. He lifts my shirt to caress my belly, and I let out a soft moan of longing. His fingers trail slowly up, his hand rising to cup one of my breasts, and then the other. I buck against his touch each time, and he soothes me by kissing the side of my neck, and then the top of my shoulder as he pulls my shirt back. He lifts it off, kissing the hollow of my neck, and then going lower to brush his lips against those points that wait for him. I arch my back, pressing into him as the vibration grows even stronger, becoming nearly unbearable. It travels lower, and lower still, the heat and pressure building to where I'm sure I'll explode. He reaches to undo my pants just as I reach to free him too. I pull him in tight, his desire pressing into me as we drop to our knees. We keep kissing hungrily as Esras eases me onto the grass. He keeps his eyes on mine, closing them only when the moment comes that he gently thrusts forward. I cry out with pleasure, as what I've imagined from the start finally happens. Then I close my eyes too, even as I keep seeing the stars swirling above.

CHAPTER 18

I get jolted from a deep sleep as someone grabs hold of my arm. "Get up. We need to go." It's Revlen, and she shakes me this time. "I mean it. Wake up."

I lurch upright and look around in the dark, at first unsure where I am. Then the night comes flooding back to me. Me and Esras, the two of us having sex, then laying in each other's arms, us walking back together after and quietly slipping into the house.

Okay, right. I'm in the loft.

"I don't understand," I say. "What's going on?"

"Just get moving."

Thankfully, I'm still dressed. I throw off my blanket and jump up from the mat where I've slept for the last three nights. Revlen is already at the ladder, climbing down. "If you're bringing anything, get it now."

With that, she's gone, and I scramble in the dark to find the athame. I haven't kept it strapped to my leg for days. I strap it on quickly and run for the ladder. I climb halfway down and then leap to the floor below.

The light of a candle flickers, and I can barely see as dark forms move around, forms I soon realize are Esras and Cade getting ready to go. Gylth, Tayora and Dabria stand across the room, keeping themselves out of the way.

I try again, asking anyone who will answer. "What's going on?"

"Men are riding this way," Gylth says. "They were spotted by one of our sentries."

My memory flashes back to that boy rising from the grass to run toward the village when we first approached. They must keep someone watching out there, which makes sense. I've been fooling myself to think I've been safe. No one is safe here, or anywhere in Faerie, not the way things are.

Cade and Esras stop scrambling, coming to where Revlen and I wait. We stand as a group as Gylth strides toward us through the dark. "Follow me," he says.

"What about the horses?" Esras says.

"Don't worry. We've got them."

Who the 'we' is I don't know, but I'd trust Gylth with my life. Right now, in fact, that's exactly what I'm doing. It's the other thing he said. *Don't worry.* And this time, I don't at all doubt we have plenty to worry about.

Soon, we're all but running down the street. We follow Gylth to where that street ends in a building. It's one of the larger ones, like those in the center of town. It has two wide doors, which men fling open in the dark. I can't see their faces, but I'm sure I haven't met them in the time we've been here.

One of them speaks softly. "Everything is ready."

The other closes the door. We're in darkness except for the moonlight from one window, which casts an eerie glow.

One of the men says, "Ready?"

"Yes," Gylth says.

The same man whistles softly and, across the room, another man taps his boot heel three times against the floor. He's a shadow behind sacks and barrels lined up in rows. Until this moment, I had no idea he was there.

Suddenly, the floor parts as two men push up doors from beneath. Lamps glow from where they stand beneath the earth, backlighting them. I can't see much, but I can make out that the ground ramps down past them.

"Go," Gylth says.

We move quickly down the ramp, the men above us closing the doors again. We're in a chamber, where our horses stand nickering. We climb upon them as they glance back nervously, the whites of their eyes catching what little light there is. Beyond them, a tunnel lit by torches stretches into the distance, to where it eventually tapers off into darkness.

"The sentry said they're still two miles out," a man says. "You should still have time."

Revlen flicks her reins, commanding her horse to move. "Let's go!"

*

The tunnel is long, much longer than I expected, torches lighting at best a quarter of the way. Maybe that's all they had time to light for us, or maybe they knew that by then the horses would no longer be afraid. For a while, we ride blind, relying on the instincts of our horses to carry us forward. Eventually, the ground starts to slope up again.

The horses know to stop before we know why, and I cast a sphere of light so we can see.

We find ourselves in a chamber again, dug beneath the earth, this time with wooden walls for support. I can't imagine how long it took to create these tunnels and chambers. Years, I'm sure. Possibly decades. But those who built them weren't wrong in thinking that someday they'd be needed. We wait and listen, soon hearing what we're waiting for. Our horses whinny despite our whispered assurances, as from behind the walls the horses of those hunting us thunder past.

It's the first chance I've had to ask what's been on my mind. "How did they know?"

Revlen takes the question, her gaze, as always, calm as it meets mine. "We don't know that they do."

I'm not sure what she means until Esras says, "That's true. Vintain has plenty of men, and the situation keeps growing more dire. They could be checking everywhere."

We look to Cade for his thoughts, but he remains staring into the darkness. His face is a mask of worry. I have no doubt that he's thinking of Dabria and her family.

Finally, he speaks softly. "We should go back."

"Cade, we can't," I say.

He turns to me, about to speak, his eyes bulging. I fear being the brunt of his anger, but Esras steps in.

"Going back would get them killed," he says. "That much is guaranteed."

He's right, I know, but it doesn't make things easier. I reach out, taking hold of Cade's hand as Esras dismounts to swing open the chamber doors. No one says another word as we prepare to ride again.

CHAPTER 19

We arrive back in the middle of the night, as fireballs streak across the sky and the smell of smoke drifts through the air. I have no doubt that the magic is faltering again, slipping from the Seelie grasp more and more. I feel it calling out to me, but a few attempts at performing magic of my own proves that the energy reaching me remains weak. It looks like we'll still have to rely on Sloane's amulet, at least for a while, and Revlen uses it to disguise me with a glamour. We can't risk having me be seen, and we can't risk being seen with Esras, who separates from us before we enter the city.

Cade too departs, going back to Silvermist. He does so at Revlen's request, maybe because she wants to get a sense of things there, or because Dabria's hopes raised her own. I'm not sure. Much of the time, Revlen keeps her thoughts to herself. Personally, I have my doubts about whether it's a risk worth taking, but Cade's committed to the cause. Either way, he promises to return in a day, and I doubt there's much that could stop him. Like a good thief, he has a knack for slipping through the shadows.

Soon, Revlen and I ride slowly through streets where no gas lamps flicker and no lights shine from windows. Clouds cover the moon, blocking most of its light. I get just one chance, when those clouds part, to see my own reflection. Revlen's glamour has once again left me unrecognizable, and this time I see a tired, middle-aged woman staring back at me. Then the clouds fill in again, leaving us in near total darkness. Which is good, since we'll be harder to see.

Silence surrounds us as we pass smoldering rubble where buildings stood before, and we guide our horses past piles of debris. But the fires that still burn, do so weakly, just small flames still flickering, suggesting that this destruction took place days ago.

We're not far from the Gilded Gargoyle, probably less than a mile, when we hear the sound of other horses. It's too late to stop or change direction, as the riders emerge from behind a corner. There are four of them, Seelie soldiers out patrolling the street. We trot slowly toward them not knowing if there's still a curfew. If so, we could be killed on sight.

They draw closer but don't reach for their swords. So, either the curfew is no longer in place or these men don't care. As Esras told us, many of the Seelie don't approve of what's happening. Most, in fact. Maybe these four, sent out to face the risk alone, feel just as trapped as the Unseelie. Or maybe they just don't see us being enough of a threat.

Still, they stare as we ride toward them, and we keep our eyes fixed straight ahead. I can only pray that the glamour is holding.

"You shouldn't be out," one of them says, but without conviction.

We nod and Revlen says, "We were just going home."

Then another says, "Stop."

We have no choice but to comply. They have swords and we have hidden knives. I've never trained for fighting and our magic is weak, which leaves just Revlen to defeat four Seelie soldiers.

The one who issued the command looks us up and down with weary eyes. When he says nothing more, I think he's about to tell us to keep moving. Then he turns to look at me again, his eyes narrowing. Can he somehow feel the magic Revlen cast to disguise me?

"What's your name?" he says.

I hesitate, unsure what to say. We should have thought of something beforehand.

"I said what's your name."

Suddenly, he bucks forward with his back arched and his arms thrown out. He gasps for air, his eyes bugging as he gurgles up a spray of blood. I spot the arrow shaft protruding from his back just as another pierces his neck. He topples from his saddle as his horse rears up, whinnying in fear. The other soldiers look around wildly as more arrows slice through the air, missing them but not by much. We're forgotten as they take off at a gallop, within seconds riding away.

That was us last week, I think. We were the ones running and hiding. And while I fear for the safety of Dabria's family, hoping nothing bad happened to them in that raid, I suspect we would have been returning here soon anyway. It can't be long now until things shift. As if to underscore that point, when I look up another fireball streaks through the sky.

*

Revlen lets the two of us into the Gilded Gargoyle, using the street entrance since there was no need to skulk through alleys or use the hidden door. We didn't encounter another soul. I soon learn that there are several more rooms beneath the bar. Some hold weapons, others supplies, and some are intended for places to meet, hide or recover. The bar itself is a front, of course, while what's beneath it serves as both a rebel headquarters and safe house.

"There are many such places in Gorgedden," Revlen explains. "Beneath both homes and businesses. They've been constructed over time, and we've had plenty of it."

"Cade showed me the sewer tunnels," I say.

Revlen chuckles, most likely thinking of the smell. "And, of course, the sewers. I started out running messages through those tunnels."

Within my mind, I picture a little girl. She has dirty clothes, oily hair and one eye. She runs through sewer water risking her life, when months ago she would have been home in bed.

"Would you like something? Wine or beer maybe?"

I shake my head. "I think I'm okay. Thanks."

By which I mean I need to rest.

Revlen and I descend the stairs to the level below, where she unlocks the door to the room I'll be using. "Try to get some sleep."

I glance at her to see if she's joking. I'm exhausted, perhaps more so than I've ever been. We barely stopped riding for two days, subsisting almost entirely on strips of smoked meat. When we slept, we did so on the ground and not for long.

"You do the same," I say.

She turns and walks down the hall, striding with cat-like grace. In the short time I've known her, she's never once seemed tired. She seems perpetually watchful and ready, and I suspect she's remained so since she was ten. I don't wait to see which room she goes into. If Revlen wanted me to know, she'd have told me.

I close the door behind me, realizing that the room I'm in is the same one where I spent that first night with Esras. Part of me wonders if Revlen put me there deliberately, so I can feel close to him while he's away. I suppose it could be a coincidence, but I don't think so. Revlen doesn't miss much, and I doubt my return to the loft late the other night went unnoticed. She doesn't strike me as being sentimental, but I don't suppose life has afforded her that luxury. All the same, I appreciate the gesture.

I peel off my clothes, wrap myself in a blanket, and stretch out on the sofa. I heave a grateful sigh at the feel of cushions beneath me. Almost immediately, sleep starts to carry me off, and I surrender to it, imagining myself being next to Esras.

CHAPTER 20

In the dream, we sit before the fire behind Dabria's house. I look past those flames into the darkness, as it becomes a tunnel lit with flames of its own. I get up and start walking, alone now, drawn toward a light at the tunnel's end. As I get closer, that light changes in shape to become a person who glows from within. Her light flickers, rising and falling to beckon me forward. I'm in one world, that of the subconscious, while my conscious mind calls me back to the other.

There's a ghost with you now, my mind says. *Wake up.*

Of course, I know, and I open my eyes to see Fashenan standing beside me. I wonder how long she's been waiting there.

I sit up and ask, "What is it?"

She stands staring, reminding me that she can only show me. I nod, letting her know I remember.

Fashenan beckons and I start to get up.

She shakes her head, and I sit back down.

"I don't understand," I say. It just comes out. I can't help it. Then I shake my head too, telling her what she already knows.

She beckons again, this time holding her palm out flat to stop me. It makes no sense. She wants me to come with her, but not move? Suddenly, instinctively, I realize what she's trying to say, as those words I read about Sativola come back to me. *She could step out of her body and walk with the dead.*

I shake my head. "I can't do that."

Fashenan might not understand my words, but she knows what I mean. She nods slowly, but repeatedly.

Can she know somehow what I am? Who I might be connected to? It would seem so, since she beckons yet again. The same way, with her palm held out.

I keep my eyes on hers. "You'll have to show me."

It can't be my words, so it must be that I don't try to rise this time. Fashenan steps forward and takes hold of my hand. Like last time, a chill runs through me, not from fear but from making contact with spirit. She's alive, but not physical. Hers is a flesh without blood or warmth. She closes her eyes and remains that way. When I do nothing, she nods. Somehow, I understand. She wants me to close my eyes too. I do, at first seeing only darkness, and then the glowing blue spot where we touch. At first, it pulses like an orb, that source where our energies meet. Then the light spreads to take on her form again, glowing brighter now, more vibrant as I see her without using my eyes. Without letting go, Fashenan steps back, taking me with her as I leave my body. My feet move without feeling the floor.

I can't help it, and a gasp escapes my lips, followed by a surprised and frightened laugh. I can hear myself, but I can't be heard, except by very few. I know this now, as I spin around to see myself still sitting on the sofa. It should be shocking, terrifying, but it's not. In fact, I've done this before, as a child when my body was taken. There was that short time, before I found Julia, during which I wandered as a ghost.

Suddenly, I realize something else. Autumn did the same, she told me. She stepped beyond her body when, for her too, it was the only means of escape. Until now, I've imagined that being the connection, but suddenly I know the truth. For both of us, it was trauma that forced us to do this thing, for which trauma isn't required. We're veil witches. It's within us to do this. It is, in fact, part of our legacy.

She could step out of her body and walk with the dead.

Fashenan moves forward, starting to flicker, while I keep trying to follow on foot. She turns and beckons again, almost impatiently this time. As if to say, "Here, let me show you," she reaches out once more to take hold of my hand. This time, we rise from the ground. She turns to look at me, her fierce eyes staring into my own. The message she seems to be trying to deliver is, "Get ready."

Then she flies forward, shifting her grasp to my wrist as we pass through the wall, and then down the hall. We keep going until we're outside. Suddenly, we're flying down the street, so fast that everything becomes a blur. The sensation is both exhilarating and terrifying, as we gain such momentum that I can't perceive a thing. It's like being dragged with incredible force through a tunnel, without even torches lighting the way.

In the moments that pass, I remember Autumn telling me that she too at first assumed she had to walk. Soon, she learned that just thinking of someplace could take her there. Part of me wonders if right now, despite how fast I think we're moving, I'm forcing Fashenan to move slowly. I can't think of where she's trying to take me, so my thoughts can't take me there.

Finally, we start to slow. I can see what's around me again and I gasp as I look down, realizing we're in the sky. Beneath us, moonlight shines down on houses surrounded by walls. As we keep moving, the houses grow larger, the lands surrounding them more vast. We must be above where the nobles live. Before long, I catch a glimpse of familiar grounds, an estate with gardens holding topiaries large enough to be seen from the air. I think we might be travelling to Fashenan's own house—if, in fact, she still thinks of it that way— but we don't stop. Soon we swoop in low over an estate so grand that it could only be one place. Flags flutter from towers. Guards patrol both within and outside the walls. The palace. It has to be.

My stomach plunges as we suddenly plummet, and then we're inside, flying through halls lit by magic and lined with gold-framed paintings. Suddenly, we come to a stop so abruptly that it would seem in defiance of physics. But it's not, is it? Only in the physics of the world I know.

We're behind a man who strides down a hall. His boots click against marble floors, and his black cape billows behind him. He's tall, thin and purposeful, with long bone-white hands adorned with rings. He wears his platinum hair loose, and it cascades to his shoulders, with just the points of his ears poking through. I don't have to see his face to know who he is. I bristle at the sight of Vintain, disgust and hatred rippling through me.

He reaches the end of the hall, where two guards swing open doors at his approach. He enters a vast chamber with vaulted ceilings and rows of slender arched windows reflecting the light of torches. The center of the room is devoted to a massive table of gleaming wood so dark that it's nearly black. At its head, sits a woman. She too is tall, thin and pale. She wears a green velvet dress and has silver white hair. Upon her head rests a delicate crown rising in a series of points. I expected Queen Abarrane to be old, and I suppose she must be, but her porcelain skin shows barely a line. She's also stunningly beautiful, but in the way of something not real. It's a frightening beauty, as if she's more a carved than living thing.

At Vintain's approach, she flicks her hand, barely lifting it. Two men, also seated at the table, rise immediately. Without a word, they bow and leave. Vintain neither speaks to them, nor looks their way as they pass. He goes to the table, where he stands and waits with patient confidence. Even the queen seems bored with the required formality. She flicks her hand again and he sits.

"Tell me what you know," she says, her voice soft but her tone firm.

Vintain sits back and crosses his legs, one over the other. "She hasn't returned to her realm. Of that I'm certain."

A chill runs through me at his words. How much more have their changelings learned about me since I've been gone. Are they watching my friends and family? They must be for him to know that.

"That only tells me where she isn't." Queen Abarrane says it without reproach, although a hint of annoyance shows in her pale green eyes.

Vintain nods, acknowledging the criticism. "We have men searching the outpost villages."

The queen sighs. "We should have flooded those ant hills decades ago. Have they discovered anything?"

Vintain hesitates, just slightly, and then shakes his head. "Not yet."

At this, relief washes over me. I can't be sure, of course, but nothing indicates that Dabria, her family, or their village came to harm. That's as much time as I have to think, before Vintain continues.

"If she did take refuge within this realm, and I believe she did, then she must have found someone to help her."

The Queen swivels her head his way. "Other than the half-blood you spotted before."

Vintain nods. "Yes."

"And you're certain she isn't in Silvermist."

I wait for Vintain's answer, thinking there's no way for him to know. The fae can't go to Silvermist, nor can they put changelings there.

"We're certain."

My blood runs cold at what his words imply. He can't possibly know, but somehow he does.

"And this help you believe she's found. Presumably, you mean the rebel faction."

It's the first time Queen Abarrane shows agitation. Her long fingernails tick on the table's surface, like a stopwatch counting the seconds.

Vintain seems to observe the same, his eyes traveling to where the queen's nails mark the passing of time. "Most likely, yes," he says. "I can't imagine any others being willing to take the risk."

"Then step up your efforts. I expect you to find her."

"Of course."

Queen Abarrane dismisses Vintain with a flick of her hand. He stands, bows and walks toward the door.

"And Vintain," the queen says.

He stops.

"You said you suspected there might be a psychic bond between the witch and her friend."

He nods, his hands clasped behind his back. "I believe they sense when the other is in trouble, or in pain. But the girl can't possibly know where her friend is."

"I don't care," the queen says. "Step up your efforts there too."

"Of course," Vintain says, and then he resumes walking.

*

White hot rage washes over me as Vintain leaves and the queen remains at her table. I have no doubt what that last exchange meant, and I'm not sure which one of them I want to kill more—the queen for suggesting he torture Julia, or Vintain for being so casually willing to do so. My gut twists with anger and frustration, and I stand paralyzed until Fashenan reaches out to me again.

She's right, of course. There's no reason to remain. It will do us no good.

"Do you know where she is?"

Fashenan may not understand my words, but my tone must convey my meaning. She nods, takes hold of my wrist, and we drop through the floor—one level, and then another, and yet one more. Almost instantly, we stand in another long hallway, this one lined with only white doors. Somehow I know just by looking that they're locked and that this must be where they keep the changelings. Fashenan points to a door, while making no move to join me. She leaves me to see what I asked to see.

I pass through the door, into a small cell of a room. Moonlight glows weakly from a slit of window up by the ceiling. In that dim light, I see Julia sitting on a bed, hunched forward with her legs crossed beneath her. It's impossible to know whether she just woke up, hasn't slept, or time has become lost to her. She stares out with a flat and distant gaze. She's sickly pale, as if she hasn't been outside for weeks. The room is blank, its walls and surfaces bare, utterly devoid of anything personal. There's just the bed on which Julia sits, a dresser, a small round table and a hard wooden chair. They've given her nothing, not even paper on which to write. How long have they left her this way?

I speak softly, my breath catching in my throat. "Oh, Julia."

I expect her to sense my presence, to look my way, but she doesn't. She remains rigid, a vision of despair.

I go to her, reaching out but afraid to startle her. Would she even feel my touch? In the past, I would have guessed yes. Hers is a world of emotional impressions, of empathy and intuition, as much as anything else. Now, I can't be sure.

I try again. "Julia, it's me."

This time, she speaks softly, barely above a whisper. "Cassie?"

She doesn't turn or look around, as if she no longer trusts her inner senses, the very thing that makes her what she is. It could well be that, in this realm, those senses are lost to her.

"Yes, it's me. I'm here with you."

Slowly, she shakes her head. She whispers, "I'm imagining you, aren't I? You can't help me."

I reach for her this time, touching her shoulder. "Julia, I'm right here. Please believe me."

Again she shakes her head, a tear escaping her eye to trickle down her cheek. Then she lays down on her side, tucking her legs up and wrapping her arms around them.

I kneel beside her, grasping her shoulder. "I'm going to get you out of here. I swear it."

Julia stares a moment longer, her gaze fixed on nothing, and then she closes her eyes.

CHAPTER 21

The first thing I become aware of are the voices upstairs, once again coming to me muffled and distant. Again, a murmuring mix of both male and female. I open my eyes and strain to listen, thinking I might hear Esras among them. My mind flashes back to that first morning here, when I woke up in this same room. For just a moment, I wonder if I could have dreamt last night's experiences. Then seeing Julia comes back to me. Maybe I could imagine the queen's inhuman beauty. Or even the words she exchanged with Vintain. But no dream could deliver the despair I felt emanating from Julia, nor the crushing sorrow I felt in her presence. That was real. I felt it in my core, even as I feel it now.

As I did last night, I wonder how Fashenan knew where to find her. How could she know which room held her? I can only assume that the knowledge was gained beforehand, when Fashenan went spying within the palace. Chances are, I'll never find out, but I once again marvel at what the dead sometimes know. We left after that, the return a dizzying blur during which I could barely think. Perhaps it was a kindness that somehow, with its essence gone, my body had laid down and gone to sleep. Returning to that sleeping body was the only thing that allowed me to rest. Otherwise, sleep would have been impossible.

Now, I rise and walk down the hall. I climb the stairs to find Revlen seated at her table beside Esras and Cade. Ecubon, Tonorf and Verin have also returned. I have yet to pass a window, but I'd guess that at best the sun has just started to rise. It would seem that Queen Abarrane and Vintain weren't the only ones up before dawn. I go unnoticed as I stand in the doorway.

"What we suspected is true." Verin addresses the group, her focus mainly on Revlen. "Their men are demoralized and poorly trained. They've grown lazy in the time that's passed."

"They've relied entirely on magic," Tonorf says. "Without it, they'll be lost."

I'm right there, but their voices sound a mile away as I continue to think of Julia. I keep seeing her sitting in that room, desperate, alone and hopeless. Queen Abarrane's words echo inside my mind. *There might be a psychic bond between the witch and her friend. Step up your efforts there too.*

"At this point, their troops are fragmented," Ecubon says. "Half of them keep trying to maintain order, while the rest remain holed up at the palace. They never thought this day would come."

Is Vintain, at this very moment, preparing to torture Julia? And is he right about our connection working that way, in his hope to lure me in? Will I know if she's in pain? In the past, it's always been she who has known when something happens to me. I've always been too headstrong, too preoccupied with my own thoughts and actions, to know when something happens to her. In a word, selfish. Which is what brought this upon her to begin with.

"It's as we thought, then," Revlen says. "Clearly, something has destabilized the ley line. It's been in flux for a while, but nothing like this."

"It's almost like it's reaching out," Verin says. "Seeking something to finally tip the balance."

Esras's gaze drifts to me, where I remain in the doorway. "Or someone," he says.

All eyes turn my way, as the others become aware of me too.

"Good morning," Revlen says. "Did you manage to get some rest?"

I nod, but don't move toward the table.

Cade cocks his head. "Cassie, are you okay?"

"I'm fine," I say.

I can't bring myself to tell them about what I experienced. Not yet. I'm still too raw, too unsure of what to do, even as every fiber of my being screams out for me to do something. "I think I'll step outside and get some air."

The truth is, I don't really feel the need to get some air. God knows, it probably smells of smoldering fires out there. But I keep seeing Julia's face before my eyes, her vacant expression and her hopeless gaze. I don't want to break down in front of those gathered.

The others remain watching me, and I can see in their eyes that they know something's wrong.

"Be careful," Cade says.

"I'll stay close," I say.

I walk from the room and through the bar to stand on the empty sidewalk. It's still mostly dark out there, the sun not yet having risen above the buildings. I feel numb, tired and worried. I feel frustrated and helpless. Mostly, though, I feel my blood starting to boil, as anger rises inside me. Once again, I see that hallway lined with white doors. I imagine Vintain striding toward the one hiding Julia. Within my mind, I see her sitting on the bed, her blank expression turning to one of terror as that door opens.

My body starts to thrum, magic sparking in my veins. I feel its crackling charge, like sparks dancing along my skin. Heat spreads within my chest, and I look for a target—a window to break or a wall to smash down—anything upon which to vent my rage. Just as quickly, the energy withdraws, as it's suddenly cut off again. I ball my fists and dig my nails into my palms, as I let out a cry of frustration and rage.

Suddenly, a woman shouts, "Cassie, look out!"

I spin at the sound of her voice, just as someone comes at me. I barely have time to register a figure, dressed in black. A man, I think. Tall. I see the quick glint of a blade. In the same instant, someone else barrels past me, slamming into the stranger and taking him down. Two shadows spin in the dirt, struggling for control of the knife. I hear grunts, blows striking flesh, and the labored breaths of their struggle. For just one instant, the stranger gets on top, and I realize it was Esras who ran past me. Then he regains control, flipping the other man onto his back.

Suddenly, the stranger lets out a strangled groan. The struggle stops as his limbs go limp.

Esras leaps to his feet, backing away as he draws in breaths. I look past him to see the other man, where he lays upon the ground. The sky continues to brighten as he stares up, his bloodied hands wrapped around the dagger hilt protruding from his chest. In that same instant, a beam of sunlight clears the rooftops to shine on his face. My eyes widen in disbelief. The man who came at me was Isaac.

Everything happened so fast that I've all but forgotten the woman who called out to warn me. She runs past me now, dropping to her knees at Isaac's side. It's Sloane, tears streaming from her eyes as she reaches out to her friend with shaking hands.

"What were you thinking?" she says. "Isaac, why?"

His eyes bulge as he tries to raise himself up on his elbows. He labors to breathe as he tries to speak, his voice little more than a whisper. "We can't let them get the key," he says. "Please listen to me. We can't let them—"

Isaac sucks in a breath as his eyes roll back in his head. What strength he had left leaves him, and he slumps back to the ground, his hands losing their grasp on the knife. Beside him, Sloane sits on her knees, folding in on herself as she weeps. Her back shudders as she softly repeats her friend's name over and over, her voice numb with incomprehension.

In my shock, I only now become aware of Esras, who has come to stand beside me. I feel his eyes upon my face, checking to see if I'm okay. But I keep my gaze on what only I can see. I watch as Isaac's spirit rises from his body, a bluish white shimmering orb that quickly fades from the realm of the fae.

CHAPTER 22

"It's time to make our move," Revlen says. "We've never experienced anything like this, and we'd be fools to waste the chance."

To make her point, she raises her hand and a blue electrical glow rises from her fingertips. She passes sparks between them like a magician performing a coin trick.

"It's true," Ecubon says, cradling within his own hand a burning flame. "We're getting our magic back. This has never happened before, no matter how much the Seelie seemed to be losing control."

My ears prick up at his words. Until this moment, I've wondered but I've never been sure. Now I know that my experience truly has been different from theirs. Even though my magic here has kept slipping in and out of my grasp, it's kept fighting to get through. But what does it mean, and why am I different? And while right now, I can feel magic pulsing through me, I also know that doesn't mean it won't soon be cut off. Only one thing seems clear. Each shift gets stronger, and this feels like the strongest one yet.

"Which is not to say they won't retain magic of their own," Revlen reminds us. "It only means we may finally have something like a level playing field. And even that's a stretch."

As we sit gathered at the table, I remind myself to pay attention. I'm in this game and the stakes are high. Very high. At the same time, it's a struggle not to remain numb from the shock of what happened earlier. The same thought keeps going through my brain: Isaac tried to kill me.

Whether it was Isaac who tried those other times, I'm not sure, although I suspect that was probably the case. Cade, I can tell, is struggling to focus too. He keeps slipping away, his expression haunted with the knowledge of what he's learned about his friend.

After it happened, we brought Sloane back to the Gilded Gargoyle, while Revlen and her people went to retrieve Isaac's body. We did what we could for Sloane. Eventually, she told us how she became suspicious of Isaac weeks ago, but had remained more so after their argument. In fact, he'd been acting strangely since Cade first told them about my ability to cross into Faerie, at the time voicing his speculations to his partners. Even then, he'd wondered if I might be the one described in that passage he'd also learned about through Kezia.

After that, Sloane observed that Isaac became uncharacteristically quiet whenever Cade mentioned me. Even as he listened intently, as if noting every detail of my comings and goings. In the time that passed, and as Isaac more frequently voiced his concern about the fae possibly finding their way back into the human realm, Sloane began to wonder.

Last night, when Cade came back to Silvermist, Isaac became especially agitated. According to Sloane, he didn't sleep after Cade went back to his apartment. Instead, she found him sitting in their darkened living room. The feeling she got was that he might be listening. And when she heard Cade set out this morning to make his way back, she checked to find that Isaac had left too. She concluded that he must have followed Cade, and she did the same.

As for Esras, he became concerned earlier when I came upstairs. Like Cade, he noticed that I seemed distracted and upset. He'd also wondered if I was safe being outside. He came to check on me just in the moment that Isaac and Sloane both appeared. If he hadn't, I'd likely be dead.

But all of that is over now. Isaac is dead, Sloane has returned to Silvermist, and major shifts have been happening with the ley line in just the last few hours. Revlen is right. The time is now, which means I need to get my act together.

"Here's what's going to happen," Revlen says. "Cells throughout the city will start creating disturbances in the next couple of hours—coordinated events to call out the Royal Guard and start spreading them thin. At this point, the Seelies have outed themselves. We know they're nowhere near as many, nor as strong, as they've led us to believe. We're estimating that at least half their forces will become bogged down in crowd control. Don't get me wrong. We don't expect to win in one round, but we do think our proud Queen Abarrane will send her men out hoping to set examples. In doing so, she'll continue to demoralize her troops. They're nowhere near ready for a fair fight anymore."

Revlen brings her attention to bear on Ecubon, Tonorf and Verin. "Each of you will lead your factions toward the palace. Tonorf to the west wall and Verin to the east. Ecubon and I will lead the charge toward the main gate."

"I'll ride with you," Esras says.

A moment of silence follows. "I'm not sure," Revlen says. "It might work to our advantage if—"

"I'll ride with you." Esras repeats, keeping his eyes on hers. The message is clear. He's done with hiding the fact that he has taken a side.

Revlen nods. "Very well. If you're sure."

"I am."

Revlen turns to me and Cade. "Cade, you'll take Cassie through the tunnels. I trust you remember their layout well enough."

Tunnels? This is the first I've heard of it, but it isn't like I've ever been sure how I could rescue Julia from her prison. My astral reconnaissance with Fashenan was definitely informative, but stepping out of my body again won't allow me to help her.

A smile tugs at the corner of Cade's mouth. "As long as Cassie can take the fragrance."

Oh, *those* tunnels. I look at Cade to make sure I understand correctly.

He shrugs, indicating that I do.

Great, so that's our game plan. Everyone heroically charges the walls, while rebel cells create diversions throughout the city. Meanwhile, Cade and I scuttle like rats through the sewers. Was that part mentioned in any prophecies? Something tells me probably not.

*

We spend the next few hours biting our nails and waiting, while Revlen dispatches messages to cells throughout the city. As she prepares, I see my first lingualawks, sleek silver birds with sky-blue eyes. Revlen whispers words into their ears, as the birds sit perched on a wall in the alley. They take to the air one by one, rising into the clouds where they become nearly invisible.

Soon, it's just a matter of time until all hell breaks loose. The impression I get is that, while the Seelie know about the rebels, they've never taken them seriously. They've long regarded any opposition as having no teeth. Which has largely been true until now. As a result, they've failed to notice not only the extent of the rebel movement, but also the fact that they've been quietly training for years.

Finally the moment comes for those attacking the palace to ride out. Before long, the streets will flood with rebels approaching those walls, while in other parts of the city they'll confront soldiers representing the crown. I have no doubt that Revlen is correct in her assessment. More than likely, they won't overthrow the Seelie regime in one fell swoop. Still, the pandemonium about to bloom will serve as a vivid wake up call. Unless the Seelie can regain their stranglehold on magical power—something that at this point seems unlikely—their days of oppression are numbered.

As Esras joins the others to set off, he holds his head high. His eyes are clear and determined, his jaw set with conviction. All the same, I can't help but wonder if within him rages an inner conflict. He's about to take up arms against his own people—in a sense, his very own family. I can't imagine how it wouldn't be tearing him apart.

Just before he leaves, his gaze meets mine, lingering just long enough. In that frozen moment, as he straps on his sword, I receive his unspoken message. He hasn't forgotten the night we shared. He thinks of it still. Even if, in the days that have passed, there's been no way for us to be together. And, right now, it's quite possible that we'll never see each other again. Because, as strange and archaic as their methods seem, in this realm where battles are fought with magic and swords, war still means the same thing as it does in my own. People will die today, and there's no way of knowing who those people will be.

*

Soon, Cade and I make our way beneath the streets of the city—wearing, as it turns out, official palace servant uniforms. Not exactly what I had in mind, and definitely not the stuff of prophecies. At least to my way of thinking. Essentially, these are the same types of clothes worn by those serving the Ferndelm family—a plain, sturdy skirt and blouse for me, wool pants and collarless shirt for Cade. The only exception being our leather vests bearing the crest of the Winter Court. Yes, I'm feeling more heroic by the moment, especially now that I'm dressed as a medieval scullery maid.

The clothes were somehow procured by one of Revlen's people, the idea being that we'd have a better chance of going unnoticed. I'm also wearing a glamour Cade cast, one fitting the part. A quick look at myself showed me to be a young woman with frizzy auburn hair, freckles and hazel eyes. Let's hope it lasts this time.

As far as the sewers go, we're far from the only rats scuttling along. While I imagined it being just the two of us stumbling through the stench-filled darkness, the tunnels are ablaze with torches. Unseelie men and women move past us in both directions, on missions of their own. Before long, we cut away from the main flow as we enter another tunnel through which we alone move. My heart starts racing at knowing that ours is a singular objective. We alone will attempt to enter the palace grounds.

I can't help but give voice to my fears, only now asking what I should have before. "Cade, is this a suicide mission? Would we be better off waiting?"

Even as I speak the words, I regret them. Julia remains trapped and terrified. How can I even think about waiting?

"Look, I'm scared too," Cade says. "But, no, I don't think it's suicide. Revlen's right. If too many of us tried getting into the palace, we'd be spotted immediately. *That* would be suicide."

I nod and keep trudging along. "I guess that makes sense."

"Besides, the Seelie don't want to kill you," Cade says. "They want to capture you."

"Thanks for reminding me."

Cade laughs. "Sure thing, buddy. If it helps, try thinking of this as a heist."

"A heist."

"Exactly. We slip inside, steal your friend, and slip back out of there again. Piece of cake, right?"

"Except for the part about it being a heavily guarded palace protected by the realm's most powerful mage."

Cade makes a scoffing sound. "Every heist has some complications. Try not to worry."

I stare at Cade's profile, but he doesn't crack a smile to signal that he's kidding. He is kidding, right?

We continue slogging along for another half hour. Thankfully, there's not as much sewage down here as I remembered, and the stench is way less intense. Maybe the Unseelie drained the sewers for today's subterranean activities, or maybe we just got lucky. Either way, that part is good. Okay, it's the only part that is, but I guess I should take note of whatever there is to be thankful for. At least if we're marching to our deaths, we won't go out reeking too badly. Hey, no one can ever say I'm not an optimist.

"Okay, this is it." Cade stops and points at one of the rusty ladders lining the slick stone walls. "At least I think it is."

"You think it is?"

Cade shrugs. "Hey, burglary isn't an exact science."

Involuntarily, I ball my hands into fists. "Yeah, Cade. I'm pretty sure burglary is supposed to involve a certain amount of precision."

"And it does." He gestures at the ladder again. "I'm at least eighty percent sure that will take us up to the palace grounds. Those really aren't bad odds."

Given that Cade's assessment of us having found the right location involves a twenty percent chance of failure, I'm definitely afraid to hear his opinion of our overall chances for success. I decide we've probably had enough conversation and start following him up the ladder.

CHAPTER 23

Cade reaches the top and lifts the sewer cover a crack to peek out. "I was right," he whispers. "Now let's move quick."

He scrambles up and out, and I do the same. We're literally in the middle of a street, which leaves me confused, but there's no time to think. Cade sets the cover back in place and we make a dash for nearby bushes.

"We should be near the gardens," Cade says, once we're reasonably hidden.

"Should be?"

"We are," Cade says. "At least I'm pretty sure."

Fair enough. This is the palace, after all. I can't imagine he's ever been here before. At least we made it to our destination. Meanwhile, I survey our surroundings to see that I wasn't wrong about my initial impression. We really did just exit the sewers through a manhole cover in the middle of a street. And I guess it makes sense that they'd have manholes in Faerie. Or faeholes, or whatever. Someone must have to work in the sewers occasionally for legitimate purposes, and not be down there just because they're either plotting or stealing. But I didn't realize there would be streets within the palace grounds, although I guess that too makes sense. From what I saw the other night with Fashenan, the palace grounds looked to be enormous.

At the moment, the street appears to be empty, a peaceful scene compared to everything else. Above us, fireballs streak through a sky that has grown suddenly dark, as if a bad storm is rolling in. Bells ring from several towers while that same high pitched alarm from the other night shrieks through the air. In the distance, men shout, the sound of their confusion punctuated by explosions rocking the ground. We were underground for less than an hour and it feels like the entire world has changed.

I turn to Cade, trying to keep my voice low. "What do we do now?"

He jabs a thumb over his shoulder. "See that giant house over there? We need to get inside it and find your friend while Abarrane and her idiots are looking the other way."

I look in the direction he just pointed to see that the palace really isn't too far off. Maybe a quarter mile or so. I try to look at it his way. It really is just a giant house. Well, a mansion, but still. And I already know where they're keeping Julia. On top of that, I can feel magic surging through me again. That alone changes everything. Now, we just have to hope that Revlen's plan works and the Seelie soldiers are too distracted and spread thin. Armed with magic, Cade and I should be able to handle a few on our own.

"I'm ready when you are," I say.

"You're sure?"

"I'm sure, Scamper." And I figure I better ask while I still can. "By the way, in case we die, what the hell does that even mean?"

A crooked smile appears on his face. "It's from an Unseelie children's story."

I didn't see that one coming. "A children's story?"

Cade's smile keeps growing. "Yep. About a thief who stole from the rich and gave to the poor."

A grin spreads across my face too. "Seriously, Robin Hood?"

Cade shrugs, but I can tell he's kind of proud. "Yeah, same deal, basically."

"Wow, Cade the hero," I say.

On one hand, having this conversation right now makes absolutely no sense. On the other, this moment of levity might do us good before heading in. We both know that anything can happen. Despite Revlen's plans, the odds in our favor aren't particularly good. It's just that neither one of us can bring ourselves to admit it.

We get moving, to find that Cade is right about the gardens being nearby. We soon cut behind a row of massive hedges and from there onto paths not unlike those I wandered behind Raakel's house. No, I can't bring myself to think of it as Esras's house, or Fashenan's. Not even Luchtane Ferndelm's. That house of sadness and cruelty was created by Raakel, and I'll never think of it as belonging to anyone else.

As more fireballs streak through the darkening sky, it's a surreal experience to make our way through the most beautiful garden I've ever seen. Roses of all colors fan out in giant swaths beside us. The blooms are truly unearthly in size, infused with a health that could only have originated in magic. Beside those are huge beds of tulips, ranging in colors unparalleled on Earth. Butterflies the size of kites float peacefully through the air, while equally large dragonflies flit past, their wingspan a seeming contradiction to their gossamer fragility. We pass topiaries dwarfing anything on the Ferndelm estate, many shaped like dragons, reminding me that somewhere behind this display of opulence yet another creature remains imprisoned.

That I should care makes me wonder just how much my sensibilities have changed in the last few weeks. After all, the only time I've seen the dragon was when it was hunting people down. But I haven't forgotten what Cade told me. That dragons, left to themselves, bother no one. Nor have I forgotten what Revlen said when I asked how the dragon was kept. *You wouldn't like it. Not from what we hear.*

Our heads jerk up at the sound of hooves pounding the earth, and we dash behind a topiary just in time. Troops on horseback race past as more explosions sound in the distance. As if answering that call of violence, the sky flashes with lightning, great jagged arcs shooting toward the ground. We wait until we think we're safe, and then start moving again just as a giant tree before us gets struck. It bursts apart with an earsplitting crack. The sweet fragrance of the garden becomes lost to the acrid smell of smoke drifting our way, both from the burning tree and fires raging beyond the walls.

Startled to stillness, we set out again, but we don't get far before a Seelie soldier appears on the path. He looks nearly as stunned at seeing us as we must appear at seeing him. He recovers quickly, placing his hand on the hilt of his sword.

"What are you two doing out here?"

Neither of us say anything. Instead, I pull up my magic, willing it to rise before he draws that blade. The current hums through my veins.

The guard looks back and forth between us again, this time glaring. "Servants are to stay inside. I could take your heads for this. Do you realize that?"

In that moment, I see him for what he is. I've rarely encountered any old looking fae, but he looks nearly seventy. Which, for a fae, means he must be ancient. He's probably been forgotten out here on some routine patrol. The fact is, he looks scared at what's going on.

I lower the hand I'd been raising to strike. "I'm sorry," I say. "The noise made us curious."

"Curious can get you killed." The guard gestures toward the sound of fighting. "None of this concerns you. It's just a training exercise. You should get back inside."

We walk quickly toward the house, while I feel the old man glaring at our backs. But the encounter makes me realize that wearing the uniforms really was a good idea. After all, there must be hundreds of servants on an estate this size, and to the guards we must all seem the same.

We're close now to the back of the palace, where rows upon rows of arched windows look out from an edifice of smooth white stone. But my gaze drops as I search for the windows shaped like slits. I see none, but it seems likely that those imprisoned here would be kept near the back. Like the Ferdelms, they must keep their slaves below ground, maybe off to one side of where this wing protrudes out into the grounds.

"That must be the kitchen entrance," I say, pointing to where two large doors open onto an area paved with cobblestones. While the windows are arched and decorative elsewhere, those close to the doors are simple rectangles, the doors themselves thick slabs of oak. This is the part of the house where aesthetics don't matter, only practicality for those who labor. I know the look of it all too well.

I don't check to see if the guard is still watching. My guess is that, with everything going on around us, he might well be gone. All the same, if we had a better option, it's too late to try using it. On the off chance we're still being watched, doing anything else would give us away.

We enter a kitchen easily six times the size of the one serving the Ferndelm estate, but we still draw stares. Thankfully, those stares come from servants closest to the door. Nearly all of them look frightened and curious. No, they've never seen us before, and I don't kid myself that they're fooled by our disguises. Unlike the guard, they must know who should be here. Still, I doubt one of them is going to sound the alarm. Not when survival means keeping your head down, and I can tell from their expressions that they know something serious is happening.

Sure enough, they resume their activities as best they can. Which must be a challenge, considering that the torches flicker low and none of the stoves are working. It seems like none of them know what to do, and no one has bothered to tell them. Right now, the Seelie have bigger fish to fry, but the failing lights could at least work to our advantage. Hopefully, only those closest can make us out clearly.

Now, for the next steps. Our plan is pretty straight-ahead. Find Julia without getting killed or captured, while the nobles are suddenly overwhelmed. From there, find a way to get her out of there again. Whether I'll be able to open the rift between realms for an easy exit remains to be seen. As things stand, I think it might be possible. At least, I tell myself I feel sufficient access to magic. But there's no point in trying until we achieve our objective. If realm-slipping isn't an option, then we get Julia out the same way we came in. Not the best prospect, but for now we just need to find our way down to where I saw her.

We keep making our way through the room as I scan the exits, trying to determine if any lead downstairs. I see one that seems the most likely, off to the back at the far side of the room. At least, I'm pretty sure I glimpse a stairwell as someone opens that door. Fucking hell. If I only had some sense of bearings, but last night feels hazy and dreamlike now. Still, I nod toward the door so Cade knows what I'm thinking. "Back there," I say. "That might be a way down."

Suddenly, a man's voice rings out. "Everyone, stop what you're doing and pay attention!"

He stands at the front of the kitchen, and must have just come in from the main floor. Thankfully he's not a Seelie guard, but that may not mean much. He's tall and broad-chested, standing with an air of authority although he too wears a servant's vest. He surveys the room with a scrutiny suggesting he's used to being feared.

Everyone in the room stops. They stand rigid, awaiting his next words. Cade and I too freeze in place, both of us looking down, as the man plants balled fists on his hips.

"This is a direct order from the queen. You are to remain at your posts and carry on. There will be no disruption of duties during today's training exercises."

Furtive glances are exchanged throughout the room, and it's not hard to imagine what the servants are thinking. Clearly, they can't carry on, since nothing is working. The fact that not one of them gives voice to this only serves to underscore my impression. The man who spoke may be one of them, but he's above them in station. Some sort of head servant, I guess. Either way, he's been given power, and it shows in the veins bulging at his neck and the hard set of his jaw.

He looks around the room again, his gaze challenging. "Does anyone have questions?"

I'm sure they must have a thousand, but not one of them asks. The situation is ludicrous, the room nearly dark, while outside explosions continue and alarms peal through the air.

"Very well," he says. "I will begin my inspections."

He starts walking forward, as everyone but us pretends to be doing something. They stir pots beneath which no flames flicker. They cut meat that can't be cooked. They chop vegetables beside piles that have already been chopped. Meanwhile, we remain frozen. The situation would be laughable, but I have no doubt that the man now striding through the room would happily betray us.

Wheels start creaking across the floor, and I turn as a girl says, "Can you two please help me with these?"

She's at most seventeen, pushing a cart holding pans of sliced fruit. She's thin, with dark skin and deep rings beneath bloodshot eyes. She might be half-blood, but I doubt it. In fact, she looks vaguely familiar. I get the feeling I might have seen her blurred image in one of those news articles.

I speak barely above a whisper, watching the head servant from the corner of my eye. "Of course. What can we do?"

Her hand trembles as she points to the pans upon the cart. "If you could just help me get these into the cooler."

Without another word, she pushes the cart forward. We follow, as she takes us behind tall racks stacked with kettles and pans, obscuring us from view. She opens a door set into the wall, from which a cold mist bellows.

"We keep these in here," she says.

We go first, and she follows us in, to close the door behind us. The three of us stand within the cold storage chamber. I have no idea if there's normally light in there but, right now, there's none at all. With the door closed, I hear the three of us breathing and see nothing.

The girl whispers again. "I'm Kim. Can you help me?"

Tears rise to my eyes. I just know. "You're not from here."

She takes a deep breath, barely squeezing out the words, "No. I'm…"

She stops there. I don't know why. Maybe she's afraid to say it, or maybe she can't believe this moment is happening.

"You're human," I say. "Not from this realm."

She chokes on her tears now. "Yes. Can you help me? Is that why you're here?"

I reach out and somehow find her. I grasp her wrist and say, "Yes. That's why we're here. That's part of what's happening today. I promise I won't forget you."

"Thank you. Oh, my God. Thank you."

I can barely hold it together, but I have to. "The door at the back of the kitchen. Does that lead down to your rooms?"

A moment passes while she catches her breath. "Yes."

"We need to get down there," I say. "As soon as possible."

I hear the rustling of her clothes, and I can only guess that she must be drying her eyes. "Stay in here," Kim says. "I'll knock when he's gone."

We wait in the cold, pitch dark cooler as the minutes tick past. It must be heavily insulated, since no sounds penetrate to let us know what's going on.

"What if she gets scared and leaves us here?" Cade says.

I think of the risk Kim took in helping us, and the desperation in her voice. "She won't."

Cade's whisper rises in pitch. "Do you realize the promise you just made? How are you going to help her?"

I grit my teeth and narrow my eyes, even though he can't see me. "I'll find a way."

The words have barely left my mouth when the door swings open, spilling light into the darkness. My heart jumps, but it's Kim bringing in another tray, which she slides onto a shelf. "He's gone," she whispers. "Move fast and don't talk to anyone."

Kim slips out again and we give her time before making our move. When we do, we walk briskly toward the door at the back. If anyone is staring at us, and I would imagine some must be, we don't look back. We exit calmly through the door, and then all but run down the stairs. We make it halfway when the building starts to rumble, the stairway shaking beneath our feet. We grab hold of the banister to keep from tumbling down the steps.

"What the hell?" I say.

Cade reaches out to steady me, as the entire stairwell vibrates around us. "Earthquake," he reminds me. "Just ride it out."

We don't have a choice, since doing anything else would mean breaking our necks. In those moments, a sudden and inexplicable image rises inside my mind. A vision, really, sharper and more real than any I've experienced before. I see a woman bound by chains, held within a misty void. She wears white flowing robes. Her pointed ears poke out through long blonde hair. She thrashes wildly, whipping her head back and forth as her gray-blue eyes desperately search her surroundings. What she seeks, I'm not sure, but somehow I know who she is. This time it's not Sativola. Instead, I'm seeing the consciousness of this realm's ley line. I think once again of that hidden alcove Fashenan led me toward, and what Esras told us about the Seelie magical network. That network creates the chains binding her and I need to break them.

"I think we're good."

Cade's voice cuts through, and the vision fades. I realize that the world has stopped shaking. We start moving fast, trying to make up for lost time as we run down the stairs. We finally reach the hallway and pause to make sure we're still alone. My heart hammers in my chest as I try to catch my breath.

"It's clear," Cade whispers.

I nod, wiping sweat from my brow as I send up a silent prayer. *Please, please, please let me get Julia out of here.* Even as I think it, Kim's face flashes before my eyes, and I issue another silent vow. *I won't forget you, I promise.*

215

We step out into the hall, looking around again to be sure. We see no one. Like last night, the hall is empty. Except, now, the torches flicker low while all of the doors stand open. Except one, the same door I passed through last night. It's only at this last moment that I remember. "Cade, the glamour. She won't know who I am."

Cade nods, and then reaches out to spread his hands before my face. A moment later, I feel that tingling sensation again. "There, it's gone," he says. "I'll put it back after."

We go to the door and find it locked, but we knew that would be the case. It's just a lock, and even if it's charmed that shouldn't be a problem. I call upon my magic, remembering the power I've tapped into in this realm before. It ignites within me, my chest warming as my veins start thrumming with energy. I try to ignore the fact that it's weaker than I expected. Still, it's enough for now, and a crackling ball of light blooms in my hand. I hurl it toward the door, blowing it open. Julia jumps up from the bed, her eyes wide with fright.

I want to run to her, to wrap my arms around her and beg her forgiveness for bringing this evil into her life. But there's no time for apologies or tears. "We're getting you out of here," I say.

Julia stares back in shock, her mouth still gaping. I can tell she's not sure what to believe, that she might even think she's hallucinating. Still, it's way better seeing her this way than as the hopeless, vacant girl I saw last night.

I draw in the magic again, this time calling upon it to transform the air before us, to ripple and show the shimmering. I focus with everything I have, telling myself that each time it's been me who has opened the rift between this world and our own. I'm a veil witch and I have the power to do this. Still, fear runs through me, a chilling uncertainty. Again, that image flashes within my mind. I see that fae woman struggling against her chains as they continue to tighten. I feel her desperate anguish.

Suddenly, the torch on the wall flares back to life. I tell myself this can't possibly be happening again. Not again, not now! Suddenly, Julia's eyes go wide again as she looks past me, this time her face transforming into a mask of terror.

An icy chill ripples up my spine, and I spin around to see Vintain's jade eyes and the grin splitting his face. "Hello, Cassie," he says. "Did you really think I wouldn't sense your presence here last night?"

He thrusts out his hand and the last thing I see is a bright, blue flash of light.

CHAPTER 24

My eyes flutter open and I expect to find myself in a dungeon, or strapped down in a torture chamber. Instead, the first thing I see is a massive chandelier of light green crystals. It's beautiful, actually, the most lovely light fixture I've ever seen. Of course, the fact that it glows brightly in a city kingdom powered by magic doesn't exactly cheer me up. Nor does the realization that no sounds come now from outside. No shouts, whistles, explosions or alarms. It has grown eerily quiet, suggesting peace when I know there can be none.

I'm lying on my back upon a plush velvet divan. I turn my head to see gleaming marble floors, ornate rugs, portraits framed in gold, and giant decorative urns erupting with sprays of flowers. Everything in this space speaks to opulence and comfort. In fact, it looks exactly like a room you'd expect to find within a palace. What it doesn't look like is where I expected to find myself after getting zapped by magic when attempting a changeling jail break.

I sit up and run my hand through my hair. I look around again. It seems like I'm alone, but only a moment passes before footsteps approach from behind. I turn just as Vintain walks past, not looking at me until he claims a leather chair on the other side of a massive oval coffee table topped with gold leaf. He casually crosses one leg over the other.

"So, how have you been?" he says.

I'd command my mouth not to drop open, but it's already too late. I recover after blinking several times. "How have I *been*? Are you fucking serious?"

Vintain shrugs. "Well, we were friends for a while. And, as I told you before, I don't want to hurt you. In fact, what I said stands. I truly believe our association could be fruitful."

I'm literally beyond words. All I can do is stare at him.

"Would you care for a glass of wine? Or something else perhaps." Vintain raises his eyebrows. When I don't answer, he adds, "Please accept my apologies for incapacitating you as I did. I realize it can be a bit disorienting, but I felt nearly certain you wouldn't otherwise join me for this talk."

I glare at him. "Where are Julia and Cade? What did you do to them?"

Vintain mildly shakes his head. "Not to worry. They're both fine and comfortable, at the moment in rooms right next to each other."

I'm not sure if I can believe him, but relief washes over me all the same. I feared he might immediately kill both of them upon my capture. Or, at best, toss them into some dungeon to rot.

Still, I try not to let my relief show. "And you think that's okay."

Vintain laces his fingers over one knee. "Perhaps not optimal but, as I said, comfortable enough. A temporary situation, I assure you. The fact is, their well-being is entirely in your hands."

There it is. Now we're getting to work. Fucker. "Meaning what, exactly?"

Vintain locks his eyes onto mine. "It's quite simple. You work with us, and we work with you. For example, your friends go home. Would you like to see the others returned to your realm? Not a problem. And that's just the beginning. There's way more that could be arranged. Have you even thought about that?"

It's such a curve ball that I have no idea how to respond. The best I can do is say, "What the hell are you even talking about?"

A smile tugs at the corner of Vintain's mouth. Weirdly, it reminds me of Grayson. Or him as Grayson. A smile suggesting he can't wait to share a secret. "Cassie, I get the distinct feeling that, by now, you know how hard I've worked to find you. As have others before me, for that matter. You have certain abilities which could be advantageous for us." He perches forward, both of his pale hands still clasped across his knee. "Should you choose to share those abilities, have you ever considered what it might mean for you here? Look around." He sweeps his hand through the air. "You could live like this. In fact, you could have anything you want. Think about it. You'd never have to work again. Or fear a thing. I realize it's a bit cliché, but you could live like a queen."

As he continues speaking, I feel a numbness spreading over my brain. Almost like I've been delivered a narcotic. The strange thing is, I do consider his words. I imagine never having to worry again. I picture myself surrounded by grandness and beauty.

Shit!

I shake my head, desperately trying to call upon my magic. I need to break whatever spell he's trying to cast. I feel this realm's magic reaching to me, trying to connect. Inwardly, I grit my teeth and think, *Come on! Find me! I'm right here!*

I'm not sure if any magic reaches me. All of it seems very much in Vintain's control at the moment. But my mind clears.

"I like working," I say. "You seem to be forgetting that my job consists of kicking supernatural fuckwads like you out of my realm."

To my surprise, Vintain laughs. It's another weird moment in that he laughed the same way as Grayson. With that, comes an even stranger realization. For a while, I liked Grayson. A lot, in fact. Which means I actually liked Vintain. Given what I now know, the idea makes me feel sick.

"You seem to be forgetting that, in this realm, you're the one who's supernatural. We belong here."

I glare at him. "You seem to think you're the only ones who do."

The smile fades from Vintain's face. "And you think, that as a human, you're in any position to judge? Every realm has a dominant class. Yours is no different."

Yeah, he has a point, but I'm not playing that game right now. "That still doesn't make it okay. And, by the way, each realm has a faction willing to fight for what's right. That part's the same too."

Vintain lets out a weary sigh. "And there I was hoping that the timing of your visit with today's events was just coincidental. That, just possibly, you'd simply chosen to take advantage of the distractions. But it would appear you've chosen sides."

"Obviously, the right one," I say.

Vintain nods in a manner signaling disinterest, a boredom suggesting he's heard all of that before and still doesn't care. Any memory of once liking any part of him fades, to be replaced by a freshly galvanized sense of hate.

"Well, I guess that decides it," he says. "Either way, getting to what we believe is inside you was always going to involve a certain amount of work. What remained in question was how much pain would be involved."

Whether it's coincidence or dramatically timed for this moment, I can't know, but doors at the far end of the room swing open. Queen Abarrane strides toward us, her regal head held high and her long legs carrying her forward with catlike grace. Only the slightest hint of annoyance in her cold gaze hints toward the fact that a short time earlier her entire world seemed on the verge of collapse.

Vintain, watching his queen until now, returns his attention to me. "As High Mage, I'm highly proficient in all kinds of magic. However, the High Queen holds mastery of a special kind. Try as I might, I've never quite managed to reach her level of skill."

Sweat prickles my brow at his words as my pulse escalates. There's no doubt as to who will be the target of that magic. I also suspect "magic" is much too kind of a word. I struggle to keep fear from showing in my eyes.

Queen Abarrane still doesn't look at me, or speak, as she draws close. She simply extends her arm and splays her fingers. A fiery heat envelopes me and I'm thrust into the air, where I hang like a broken marionette. She drops her arm, the burning quits and I crash down hard against the marble floor, the air getting sucked out of my lungs.

Queen Abarrane walks slowly to where I lay curled up and gasping for air. She flicks her wrist and an unseen force rolls me onto my back where I lay pinned and helpless.

Finally, she looks at me, gazing down with a sneer of utter disdain. "So, this is our veil witch," she says. "Our all-powerful veil witch, who can come and go from our realm as she pleases."

"This is her," Vintain says. His tone is similar to hers now, that of someone regarding a lower life form.

Queen Abarrane holds out her claw of a hand, quickly pulling it up. Pain sears through me as I lurch into the air again. I'm drawn up hips first, my back arched and my limbs dangling.

Queen Abarrane finally meets my eyes with her frigid gaze. "So tell me, veil witch, do you hold within yourself something of value? To look at you, I'd think it unlikely."

I can't speak or move, as I remain helplessly suspended. All I can do is narrow my eyes with hate.

Queen Abarrane laughs as she walks slowly around me. "Oh, Vintain," she says. "I believe our little trespassing mouse is angry. Do you see?"

"They're often ruled by their emotions," Vintain says. "It's part of what makes them so easily manipulated."

His words are chosen carefully, a deliberate and cruel reminder. It was those very same human emotions he used to gain my trust and affection in his attempt to ensnare me.

Queen Abarrane continues to circle me until she stands behind the top of my head. She places her hand on the crown of my skull.

"Well, on the off chance there's anything in there worth finding," she says, "I guess we better have a look."

I can't speak, but that doesn't stop me from screaming as a blistering pain shoots through me. I buck in the air, my body convulsing, as images flood through my mind. My entire life starts reeling backward, starting at this moment and flashing through every preceding moment successively. It's an explosion of imagery and emotion a thousand times too overwhelming to withstand. It feels like I'm being torn apart.

That's the start.

She digs deeper, consuming everything that I am, before going back from there into my sister's life, my mother's and my father's. I scream again and writhe in the air, while some distant part of my brain wonders how even the darkest magic will allow this. She's literally mining my DNA. Within seconds she's dug deeper yet, and I see an old woman alone in a padded cell, who becomes middle-aged, then young and then a girl. She has jet black hair, pale skin, and freckles across her nose. She's the spitting image of me and Autumn, and I instinctively know she's our most recent veil witch ancestor.

I let out another wail as I'm flayed open more, going back beyond my great grandmother, and beyond her and beyond. Queen Abarrane keeps boring deeper in a series of impressions beyond comprehension to track or consciously perceive.

Then suddenly everything stops, the images freezing to a halt as a woman comes into focus. I gasp at seeing her, that same woman who I've seen within visions and the pages of a history stolen by the fae.

Queen Abarrane purrs with satisfaction. "Sativola. There you are."

The frozen moment starts to play forward again, moving at a normal speed, and I know where we must have arrived at in time. Sativola rides on horseback across a field of battle, strewn with the bodies of men and women, both human and fae. Smoke rises into the sun as the remaining fae nobles, those who survived the slaughter, ascend upward through a shimmering rift. Sativola charges toward the closing aperture, her lips moving silently as she recites an incantation. She narrows her eyes in hate, then thrusts out her raised hand. A lightning bolt shoots from her fingers to close the final rift as thunder cracks against the sky.

Queen Abarrane's words come as a hiss. "She didn't say it. She didn't say it out loud."

I can't help it. Despite the agony, I laugh.

A searing white hot flash of pain tears through me again as she gets her revenge. "So, you think that's funny. I'm not done. I'll find it. You'll be a hollow shell before I'm through."

My suffering resumes, as the images start flickering forward again, moving by days, then weeks and months of Sativola's life. Suddenly, the visions freeze once more at a moment within which she lies upon a pallet, her hair drenched with sweat, her legs spread as she screams. Then a baby's cry rises in a room lit by torchlight. Sativola reaches out, taking the child into her arms.

"Here it is," Queen Abarrane whispers. "This is it."

In the past, Sativola speaks softly into her daughter's ear. "In the name of your father, Galen, High Prince of the Fae, he who embodied the greatness his people have turned away from, these words are yours to carry. As I speak them, they will bind with your soul, and those of our line going forward. This key will be our legacy, that I entrust to you first."

Suddenly, another voice cuts through, that of a woman I hear within me. Her voice is low, desperate and searching, just barely a whisper. *Galen. You carry the blood of Galen.*

The magic burning me alive starts to cool and wrap itself around me. I feel as if I'm being held rather than trapped suspended in a web.

"Vintain, get control of it," Queen Abbarrane says. "Now."

The other voice comes again, rising now, soothing and soft as it resonates out from my core. *I've reached out to you before. Do you remember?*

I look around, suddenly free to move my neck, as Queen Abarrane and Vintain also search the room. There's fear in their eyes, bordering on panic, and I realize they can hear her too. She's not just within me, she's all around us.

She speaks once more, her voice stronger now, louder. *You, human witch, you carry the blood of Galen.*

I recover the capacity to speak. "I don't know," I say. "I might."

Queen Abarrane's voice rises in both pitch and volume. "Vintain, you need to get this under control!"

But even her screeching is drowned out by the voice of the ley line. I see her now, her vision replacing the room around me. She's standing, the chains pooled at her feet. Her long blonde hair flows to the shoulders of her shimmering white gown. Her sky-blue eyes gaze into mine and mine alone.

Descendent of Galen, last of the true Tuatha Dé Danann, upon whom I bestowed my powers. As one of that line, you hold true claim.

Somewhere in the background, as if a million miles away, I hear Queen Abarrane's muffled scream. "Stop her! Stop her now!"

Descendent of Sativola, most noble of the witches, you are the one foretold. Fae witch, I find you worthy, and I can no longer be bound. While you remain in this realm, you alone shall access my power.

I'm gently lowered to the ground and set upon my feet, as she steps back and away from her chains. She keeps her eyes on mine, spreads her arms, and a surge of power bursts through me unlike anything I've ever imagined. It feels like each of my cells holds starlight, and that light keeps spreading outward to become me. Entrusted with her power, I hold within me not only the key to the realm, but the power of the ley line herself. Nameless because she needs none. She is elemental. She is magic. And she and I have become one.

"You have to stop this!"

Queen Abarrane's voice brings the room into focus again as the vision fades. She has her back to me as she watches Vintain, who stands within a deep cave of an alcove that was hidden behind the wall. Within it, a giant sphere spins madly above its pedestal, flickering and pulsating as it shoots out arcs of lightning, each time growing darker at its core. Vintain's eyes bulge with terror as he stands before this thing he can no longer control, or command back to his will.

I walk slowly toward them as a grin spreads across my face. Not of malice, so much as amusement. In the moments that just passed, while in the presence of the ley line, this room no longer existed. Vintain and his queen were of no concern, and they still aren't.

"Having a little trouble?"

They spin around at the sound of my voice. Neither say anything. They just stare in disbelief as I keep striding forward. Queen Abarrane is the first to recover. She locks her eyes onto mine and points her finger. I don't know if she expects to still possess magic, or for me to cower as those in this realm do before her. Neither happens.

"How dare you come here," she says. "How dare you!"

I slow my approach just a little. "Is that all you've got? Because I have to admit, this little mouse is kind of pissed off right now."

Her mouth drops open, then keeps working like a gulping fish as words escape her. I have no doubt that she's never once in her life been spoken to that way.

"You will stand away from me," she says. "You will *kneel!*"

I cock my head and frown. "Seriously? Yeah, no."

I barely have to gesture to release a rope of blue light. It lashes out, coils around her and she freezes to become a statue of Queen Abarrane, caught with her mouth gaping open.

Vintain stops his desperate attempts to bring the palace Amulus under control. He backs away from it. "Cassie," he says. "I can help you control it. I can guide you here. You could live like a—"

"A queen. Right, I know." I take another step forward. "Hey, Vintain. Remember that thing you said about not wanting to hurt me?"

He stares at me and nods, his jade eyes stricken with fear.

"Just so you know," I say. "The feeling isn't mutual."

I lash out, coil him in blue light and leave him frozen with his eyes pinned wide. I turn and start to walk away, and then look back over my shoulder . "Oh, by the way," I say. "That was for Lauren Flannery. She was a veil witch, in case you forgot. Fuckwad."

CHAPTER 25

I suspect what I'll find before I even get back to where Vintain said he left Cade and Julia. As I march through the hallways of the palace, fearless now for the first time in Faerie, I encounter way more confusion than resistance. The hallways have all gone dark, and the few guards who stand up against me go down fast. Most of them don't bother trying. It doesn't take a genius to quickly realize that I'm not Seelie, I have magic while they have none, and that I'm not in the mood to be messed with. The smart ones take off running.

Like Revlen said, the Seelie troops have grown weak, poorly trained and entirely reliant on magic. Being left to their own defenses means being close to defenseless. Yes, they have swords but, like most bullies, they lack courage. And the halls having grown suddenly dark, combined with the resumed sounds of battle outside, tells them there may not be much left to defend.

I enter the kitchen to find the head servant red-faced and screaming at the servants who remain, although it appears that half of them are gone. "What do you mean they're gone? Changelings can't just disappear!"

A woman cowers before him, her forehead glistening with sweat. "I swear it's true, sir. They just suddenly vanished."

The head servant tries again. "Don't be ridiculous! Only the High Mage can send them back!"

I walk up next to him and clear my throat. He spins to face me, seeing a prisoner he hasn't abused before. "What the hell do you want?"

"We're under new management," I say. "You're fired."

His eyes grow wide with fury. "Fired? You can't fire me, you stupid little—"

I press my palm to his forehead and he freezes mid-word, the veins still bulging in his neck. "Hold that thought," I say. "By the way, it might be a while."

I turn to the others, many of whom may have been here for years, possibly since childhood. "You guys are half-bloods, right?"

They nod, men and women of various ages wearing confused expressions. One of them speaks fearfully. "Yes, we are."

She has graying red hair, brown eyes and deep lines in her face. She makes me think of Ellie, and what she'd have ended up looking like if she'd remained trapped here.

"What about Kim?"

"She is a… was a changeling," the woman says. "She went when the others did."

A boy steps out at the back of the group. He can't be more than thirteen. "Does this mean we can leave too? I think I remember the way back to Silvermist."

I want to say yes, that they should be fine. I honestly think that's the case. Still, to be on the safe side, I say.

"Maybe wait here for a few minutes. I have a friend who can help you get back."

*

I stride down the empty hall where only two doors remain closed. The rest still yawn open, and a sense of peace flows through me at knowing those rooms won't hold occupants tonight. I go to Julia's door first. The magic holding it is no longer in place, and it opens at my touch. The room is empty, of course, as I knew it would be. There's so much I don't know about fae magic, including how a changeling can be created to begin with, but Vintain's magic can no longer hold them here. Nor can it maintain the doubles he created in our realm.

I go to the bed where Julia sat blankly staring just last night. I sit upon it, taking in the empty walls she's faced these past few weeks. Somehow, the bed still holds the warmth of her body. A tear rises to my eye, even as relief washes over me at knowing she's home again. As are the others who were taken. Of course, no one will believe their story, but there's nothing I can do. No one would believe me either. And while I can't help but wonder if Julia will ever forgive me for bringing her into this, I suspect somehow she will. The bond between us runs too deep, and we've been through so much together. In many ways, we're one.

"Hello?"

Cade's voice travels weakly through the wall. He must have heard me in here. His reluctant tone suggests that he's both afraid to ask who it is, and too curious to resist.

I go into the hall and throw his door open. "Hey, Scamper. Why are you sitting in here?"

His eyes widen and his mouth drops open.

"By the way, your door wasn't locked," I add.

He manages to find his voice. "What the hell?"

"Long story," I say. "Come on, let's get moving. Some people need your services as a tour guide, and I need to free a fucking dragon."

CHAPTER 26

I follow stone corridors and stairways as I wind my way deeper beneath the palace. There are no windows or torches to light my way, but that's hardly a problem. With this much magic now coursing through my veins, it's barely an effort to light up the halls with a blindingly bright pulsating orb.

Soon, I approach what must be the lowest level. I find no more stairways to descend, and only one long tunnel of a hall. What little air there is smells of mildew, and the stone walls drip with condensation. It's cold down here, colder than anyplace I've been in Faerie, reminding me that I'm deep beneath the ground. My breath comes out in plumes of vapor.

I keep walking as creatures scuttle away from the sudden invasion of light. They look like roaches, except they're at least a foot long and pale gray, with bulbous milky eyes. Despite their size, they manage to squeeze themselves into fissures in the stone to get out of sight. Above me, massive spider webs stretch across the ceiling. Those are inhabited by equally oversized spiders that curl in upon themselves as they too attempt hiding from the light. Shit, if I didn't have magic I'd run screaming. Even with magic, it takes everything I have to hold it together.

Finally, I see what must be the end of the corridor, and at first I think I've reached a dead end. Then I see the runes etched into the stone. No, it's not the end I've reached. It's a doorway that only the most powerful magic can open, one presumably serving as a barrier against something massive and strong. An inexplicable anger rises inside me, a rage born of the ley line and passed on to me. I let out a roar of anger and thrust out my hand. The wall explodes inward, chunks of rock shooting through the air as dust billows in the wake of that force. No, I don't need runes or incantations to open that doorway. I have no intention of closing it again.

I step over rubble into a void so dark that even the light I cast before me seems weak. I pull up more magic, increasing the force ten times at least. I launch forth a blast of light to see that I stand within an immense cavern. One, quite possibly, as old as the realm itself. At the far end, the beast huddles with its wings folded down. Its raised tail flicks at the air as it watches me with golden eyes that glow from within. It keeps its head lowered, and its mouth open to reveal rows of dagger teeth. I should turn and run, I know. The human part of my brain screams for me to do so. But something much deeper calls out to me, a force connected to this world rather than my own. Once again, I hear her voice within me.

Go to her, she says. *See what they've done.*

All the same, my blood runs cold. My heart hammers in my chest, even as I keep walking. Slowly but steadily, I make my approach.

Suddenly, the dragon raises its head high like a snake poised to strike. It tries rising up onto its legs, only to get yanked back down again by the massive chains yoked to its neck. It lets out a tortured cry and I see the cause of its pain. Blood gushes from where inward-pointing collar spikes have plunged through its scales. My eyes rivet to the creature's neck, which is ringed with scars and lacerations. Despite my terror, my heart breaks at the sight. No living thing should be treated this way. Against all sense, I run forward, thrusting out both hands to obliterate those chains.

Just as quickly, I stumble back again as the beast lurches up to full height. It spreads massive wings, flapping them to raise a storm of dust. Bones skitter across the ground at my feet, from what must have been the dragon's meals. I brace myself for a plume of fire to be launched my way. My heart pounds as I prepare to either run or defend myself with magic. But it's not me the dragon cares about. In fact, I'm all but forgotten as it suddenly lurches across the cave.

I gasp at what I see. Within a series of alcoves, smaller dragons are held bound by chains of their own. Each of them cry out, their mouths gaping as they try to extend their necks. Blood runs from their collars too, over that already crusted against their scales. Still, they try to withstand the pain, even though they can't get close enough to the one they need. They're held bound, and those recessed openings are too small for their mother to fit her head past.

For the large dragon is their mother, of course. They've enchained her babies within her view, while keeping them beyond her reach. No wonder she does their bidding. What choice does she have? I wonder how long it's been this way. Have the Seelie used magic to keep those dragons from growing? My guess is yes, and in doing so they've created a scenario of perpetual torture.

I let out another scream, this time one of fury. I thrust my hands out once more, breaking each and every chain. One by one, the baby dragons fly out into the cavern as the mother rises into the air to guide them. Still, they have nowhere to go, their cries of frustration echoing off the walls.

I march forward beneath them, part of me not even caring what happens to me. I pull up more magic, this time more force than ever before. I direct that power across the cavern to where another stone gate remains locked. That barrier shatters, exploding outward. More light floods in, a light I'm sure the dragons view as being much more magical than that which emanates from me. Because that light, although distant at the far end of a very long tunnel, comes from the sun. Daylight means freedom.

More cries echo as the excited creatures fly toward their escape route. The mother dragon circles above, herding her children out of the chamber. I breathe a sigh of relief as they disappear into the tunnel and finally she follows. Then my heartbeat kicks up a notch, and then another, as the mother spins about within the tunnel. Suddenly, she's flying back at me and I stand frozen with terror. Instinctively, I call up yet more power, this time to defend myself, even as within me a war wages. Can I possibly strike her down after what I just witnessed? And is the power entrusted to me even enough?

At the last minute, I consider turning to run, but I've waited too long. All I can do is hold my ground and decide whether to strike or not. The dragon touches down, and I nearly stagger as the ground rumbles beneath my feet. My hair blows back against the sudden gust of wind. The dragon folds in her wings and starts to advance, closing the distance between us. Her nostrils flare as she sniffs in my scent. She parts her mouth to reveal teeth as tall as me. Then she stops, lowering her head as she studies me with her amber eyes. Her pupils, cat-like slits, slowly widen, draw together, and then widen again.

Finally, she closes her mouth and lowers her head even more. She shuffles forward again. Only then do I realize what I'm experiencing. It seems impossible, but I know it to be true. While she's afraid of me, after all of the cruelty she's suffered, she's much too intelligent not to know what just happened. This gentle beast has risked more hurt to come and thank me.

I take a frightened step forward, and then one more. When she continues to wait, I finally work up the courage to close the gap between us. I reach out, and then gently run my palm against her snout. Slowly, she closes her eyes, even as her tail flicks with impatience to be gone. It's the last thing I expect, but a tear trickles down my cheek.

"Go," I say. "Please go."

The dragon needs no more. She opens her eyes again as she backs away. She keeps her gaze on mine until the distance between us is sufficient for her to turn around. Then she launches forward, one thrust of her legs propelling her halfway toward the tunnel. With just a flap of her wings she's inside and barreling toward the light beyond. A smile spreads across my face, to be replaced by a grin. An unexpected laugh bubbles up within me and I run toward the tunnel too, using my magic to fly myself forward. When I reach the end, I stand at the opening to a mountainside. I gaze out as wings, both giant and small, flap against the sunlit sky.

CHAPTER 27

The horse I took from the palace gallops toward the front door of the Ferndelm estate, where no guards stand watch now to stop me. I guess the word must be spreading fast. Then again, it's also hard not to notice when suddenly all of the magic stops working. Needless to say, it's not a great time to be a Seelie soldier, and I imagine they'll soon be the ones trying to escape through the Barrens.

I rein in the horse, hop off and go to the door. No, I don't knock. Instead, I throw it open and walk in. But, hey, I used to work here, right?

The house is silent and seems empty as I cross through the foyer and front rooms, from there past the dining room and into the kitchen. That room is empty too, the hearth black and the lights out. Food remains sitting on the counters and prep tables. For one brief moment, I think that Helen, Lily and Mitch must be gone.

Then I remember what they do in this house when the magic falters. They order their servants downstairs, like children sent to their rooms. I grit my teeth and say it out loud. "They didn't."

But I know they did.

I find them downstairs, still in their rooms and afraid to emerge. Naturally, they're confused, curious and scared. They've been down there for hours, having listened as the house above went from uproar to silence. Now, they listen with stunned expressions as I tell them that the Seelie have fallen from power. Then they stare wide-eyed as I tell them about my part in it.

Helen is the first to recover. Although, if anything, her eyes grow wider. "You possess all of the magic in Faerie?"

I shake my head, trying not to laugh, since at first I thought the same thing. "Not all of it. I suspect that would kill me. I'm just the only one who can use it right now."

I leave out the part about being juiced up like I never imagined. There's no need to brag. I also suspect that most of the magic is flowing back into where it's needed to repair the damage done to the realm.

A gleeful grin spreads across Mitch's face. "What about Queen Abarrane and Vintain? You just left them that way?"

This time, I can't resist a grin of my own. "Well, it wasn't like I had time to put them in the attic. We can figure out what to do with them later. Maybe we'll start a museum or something."

Lily bursts out laughing, covering her mouth as if she's embarrassed. "I'm sorry, but I would have liked to see that."

"Don't be sorry," I say. "I would have taken a picture if I could have." God, she's so sweet. She actually feels bad about laughing at the fate of those who ruined her life. Which is why I gladly risked my own to save her.

We start walking back down the hall toward the stairs. "What happened here?" I ask. "Where is everyone?"

"Lord Ferndelm left early this morning," Mitch says. "I was grooming the horses when he ordered me to get his ready. He seemed to be in one hell of a hurry."

Yeah, I bet. "What about Raakel?" It's impossible for me to say her name without screwing up my face, as if I bit into something sour.

"We're not sure," Helen says. "She ordered us to take food upstairs to the children, just before we were ordered to our rooms."

"I heard her tell the guards to get her coach ready," Lily says.

Helen and I seem to reach the same conclusion simultaneously. Her eyes lock onto mine. "Good heaven," she says. "Please tell me she didn't abandon her children."

For anyone else, it would seem impossible, but we're not talking about anyone else. "Did she get a new nanny?"

"Aye, Silvia," Helen says, as we start climbing the stairs. "The poor thing wandered in from Silvermist not long after you disappeared."

I'm not surprised to hear that a replacement for Ellie was quickly found, but I'm glad they trapped another half-blood this time. If the new nanny had been a changeling, the children would be alone right now. As for Raakel, I was looking forward to getting revenge, but I guess it doesn't really matter. It would be too easy anyway, and I imagine she'll get what's coming. She must have a long history of people hating her.

We come upstairs into the kitchen just as Esras swings the door open. He strides into the room, the others freezing at the sight of him.

"It's okay. He's on our side," I say, eliciting more shocked stares.

Esras rushes over and wraps me in his arms. I breathe in the scent of him, through the smell of smoke still clinging to his clothes.

"Thank the gods you're okay," he says. "Cade told us what happened."

I make the mistake of glancing over his shoulder at Helen, Lily and Mitch. It's hard not to laugh at their stunned expressions. First I put the magical hammer down on the Queen and High Mage, and now I'm hugging Esras. It must be like the whole world just flipped upside down. Which, in many ways, it did.

"I thought you might come here," Esras says. He glances at those watching us. "Is everyone all right?"

They hesitate, and then nod mutely. I wish I could tell them about everything Esras has done and been through, but that will have to wait.

"What about my family?" Esras gestures to indicate the rooms he just crossed through. "They're not here, obviously. I assume they must have fled with the rest of the nobles."

My stomach sinks at being the one to tell him. "We think the children are upstairs."

Esras's mouth drops open in shock, and the pain in his eyes makes me almost look away. Without another word, he turns and runs from the room, and I fight back the tears pricking at my eyes. For his entire life, Esras's family has caused him nothing but pain and it isn't over yet.

"Come on, guys," I say. "You should get back to Silvermist. We'll figure the rest out from there."

Helen, Lily and Mitch again seem at a loss for words. They must have dreamed of this moment a million times. For years, they've been trapped here. In Helen's case, decades. Now they can finally leave, and the reality seems impossible to process.

We leave the kitchen and start walking past all of those vast sitting rooms with their objects of art and luxury. Helen is the first to voice her thoughts. "I'm not sure where I'll go," she says. "I don't know what I should do."

I reach out and take her hand. I speak softly. "It'll be okay. We'll work it out."

We're almost through the last of the front rooms, when a figure appears in the foyer. I can't see his face in shadows, but the sick feeling in my stomach tells me who it is. That feeling is confirmed when Esras's brother emerges into the light. Despite the power I now hold, I'm momentarily crippled by my own trauma. Memories race through me of being held pinned to the ground, of his hands groping my body, of how close I came to not being able to fight him off. A recurring nightmare that I fear will always manage to take roost again.

Weylar pulls a dagger from the sheath at his belt. "Think you're going somewhere?"

I recover my senses, the power of the ley line rising inside me. I thrust out my hand, fingers spread, ready to do way more than render him immobile.

"Weylar, stop!"

Esras stands on the stairs holding Erdella, while Perth stands beside him. Behind them, a teenage girl looks back at us with wide fearful eyes. She must be Silvia.

Weylar sneers at his brother. "They're trying to leave! Were you just going to let them?"

"I was going help them, if I can," Esras says.

Weylar's face twists with disgust. "They're *half-bloods*. They're not even *Unseelie!*"

I'm so close to lighting him up, but I grit my teeth and hold back. I just can't do it in front of Esras and the children.

"It's over," Esras says. "Now put that damned knife down and let them pass."

Weylar's face turns scarlet. "What's wrong with you? You're a noble!"

Esras sets Erdella down, then starts to descend the remaining steps. "Weylar, our time is over, as it should be. In your heart, you must know this. Now, please—"

"Maybe your time is over, coward. Not mine!" Weylar spins toward us and cocks his arm back. He locks his hateful gaze on me and daylight gleams against the dagger blade.

"Look out!"

Helen's panicked shout reaches my ears in the same moment that she shoves me aside. Then she spins, her eyes

246

agape as she stumbles. She draws a ragged breath and drops to her knees, with the dagger's hilt protruding from her chest.

For one frozen moment, the children stare, their eyes wide with horror. Then Esras leaps down the stairs. He's upon his brother before Weylar has time to draw his arm back from the throw. Weylar reels against two powerful blows, the third dropping him to the floor as Esras stands over him.

I fall to my knees beside Helen, where she now lies on the floor. I wrap my arms around her, cradling her as tears stream down my face. "You'll be okay," I say. "Just hang on. You'll be okay."

Helen reaches up and gently brushes my hair back. Her voice comes out weak and soft. "I don't think so, love."

"No, please," I say. "Helen, please hang on."

I call the magic up inside me, holding onto her as I will that force toward Helen. Light blooms around her, pulsing and flickering with power. I tell myself she'll be okay, that I can make her right again. I control the magic that can help her. I reach for the knife's handle, ready to withdraw the blade from her body, believing with all my heart that Helen's wounds will heal when I do. Suddenly, the light surrounding her starts to fade. I gasp and withdraw my trembling hand as that magic continues to recede. Tears stream from my eyes as I grit my teeth and try again, willing that magic to surround her once more, to heal her. But what I want seems not to matter. For some reason, it's beyond my control, even as within me magic continues to thrum outward. The light surrounding Helen soon fades out altogether.

"Oh, Megan. You're a sweet girl," Helen says. "But some things magic just can't fix. And that's the way it should be."

My breath hitches in my throat, as my tears continue to fall. "Cassie," I whisper. "My real name is Cassie."

Helen strokes my hair again. "You'll always be Megan to me, love."

I tighten my hold on her, as I rock her back and forth. "Oh, Helen. I'm sorry."

Helen smiles at me, blood rising to the corner of her mouth. "There wasn't much for me anyway," she says. "Just look after those two. Promise me."

I look over my shoulder, to where Lily cries in Mitch's arms, both of them watching us.

I turn back to Helen. "I promise."

"You're a sweet girl, Megan. I'm glad I got to meet you." Helen gazes into my eyes one last time and whispers, "Don't cry, love. You saved me. You saved all of us."

Then I hold onto her even after she's gone.

CHAPTER 28

One month later, I return to Faerie. Not to rescue anyone this time. The mysterious rash of people suddenly changing into unrecognizable strangers has come to an end. Nor do I go because I'm compelled to join in some sort of conflict. According to what I've heard, conflicts there have ended now that magic is shared equally and only used for beneficial purposes.

Instead, I go to attend a wedding. I've brought my sister with me, traveling first through Silvermist, since I decided to keep a few secrets. One of those is that, these days, I've had to learn how to cast a glamour. It seems funny now remembering that talk I had with Helen months ago, when she told me that my ears might still grow in. At the time, I thought she was crazy, but apparently she was right. As was Sloane, who said for some it doesn't happen until they come to accept what we really are. For a while, I managed to convince myself that it was just my imagination. Until the tips of my ears started poking through my hair. Then I knew for sure that it was glamour time.

Another secret I'm keeping from my sister is that, of the two of us, only I possess the power to access the fae realm directly. Given the highly edited version of events I shared with Autumn, it seemed unlikely I could explain the difference between our powers without explaining much more. On one hand, I really do think I should tell her what happened. On the other, I know that I'll never hear the end of it.

Also, as my older sister, it burns her a little when I demonstrate magical abilities beyond her own. I wouldn't call it a jealous streak, exactly. More like we share a healthy competition. But there's no point in having her get all worked up. She'll just keep poking at me with questions until I spill the rest of the beans. So, for now, I decide to leave well enough alone.

As we take our seats alongside Lily and Mitch, Autumn keeps craning to look around. Not that I blame her, and I can barely stop doing the same. The Royal Gardens make for an exceptionally stunning wedding location, even now that the plants and flowers have shrunk to normal size and the butterflies only have two inch wingspans.

Autumn shifts in her seat again, this time for another look at the palace behind us. "I can't believe you didn't tell me about this place. It's beautiful!"

"I did tell you. We're here, right?"

Autumn shoots me a look. "You know what I mean. So, you met this Cade guy in a bar?"

"Yeah, he's the one who got me drinking pale ale." I figured that was close enough to the truth, since my first real conversation with Cade took place in the Rowan and Thistle. And I have been sampling some pale ales, so far striking out on finding anything comparable to the beer in Silvermist.

Autumn lowers her voice to a whisper. "What about the people next to us? Where did you meet them?"

She means Lily and Mitch, of course, who remain holding hands and whispering too as we wait.

"I bumped into Lily when I got split up from Cade one night. She sort of showed me around a little until I found him again."

Autumn looks at me suspiciously, but decides not to push it. People can hear us, after all. She can try to pry more out of me later.

Instead, she lowers her voice even more. "Do they normally have weddings at the palace? You said Cade's an Uber driver, right?"

A smile tugs at my lips, as it always does when I think of Cade—half-blood thief and traveler between three realms—driving people around to pay his rent. "*Was* an Uber driver," I say. "He'll be living here now. And this wedding is kind of a big deal. They just changed the law here about fae people being able to marry half-bloods."

Autumn cocks her head at that one. "Why didn't they allow it before?"

I shrug. ""Everyplace has its problems."

Autumn sighs. "Well, at least they're making progress."

"Exactly."

Having the wedding here was actually Esras's idea. For now, he and Revlen are both serving as interim leaders of Faerie. That way, both the Seelie and Unseelie are being represented until Faerie experiences its first free election in the spring. According to Cade, Esras thought it would also speak well to relations with Silvermist to hold the realm's first legally sanctioned marriage between a fae and a half-blood at the palace. All expenses paid from Queen Abarrane's coffers, of course.

As for the High Queen herself, she's been imprisoned along with Vintain and most of her Seelie court. When I heard that, I had to wonder if a prison could hold Vintain for very long. Hopefully my concerns are unfounded. After all, he can't possibly find another means of gaining access to magical power. Can he?

For now, I tell myself to relax and enjoy what's going on around me. I have to agree that having the wedding here truly is the perfect gesture. I also have to laugh since, in a way, Cade just pulled off another heist at Seelie noble expense, this time the queen herself. Well, ex- queen. It's no secret that the wedding is a gift from the kingdom, so I can only imagine that Prisoner Abarrane must be flipping out in her cell somewhere.

The orchestra, which was playing soft background music before, kicks it up a notch as the wedding party proceeds up the aisle toward their seats at the front. Revlen and Esras lead the procession, causing a murmur to ripple through the crowd. Everyone cranes to see.

Autumn whispers, "Who are they?"

I give her a quick recap on the recent shift in power, leaving out the parts involving me. So, it must seem a bit strange when, as Esras and Revlen walk by—fully decked out in their formal attire—they each look my way and smile.

Autumn grabs hold of my arm. "Oh, my God. Have you met them?"

I nod, wiggling my arm to loosen her grip. "Yeah, they're nice," I say.

Needless to say, there's no freaking way I'm telling her about me and Esras. Even now, just thinking about that night sends a ripple of pleasure through my body. I look away from Autumn, because I'm pretty sure my face just turned red.

I haven't actually spoken with Esras since leaving Faerie, although whether I left or stayed became a very close call. He asked me to stay there with him, saying now that the conflict had ended, we could finally take our time and really get to know each other. I'm pretty sure that had multiple meanings, so it was a very tempting offer, to say the least.

In the end, I decided it just wouldn't work. For one thing, I went most of my life without knowing my mother or sister. I couldn't imagine telling them I'd decided to relocate to a different dimension. There was also the fact that Esras's father, mother and brother are now in prison. His brother for murder, of course, and his parents for having held slaves. That same fate was decided for all who did since, technically, that was illegal. Sure, we might be able to get past that for a while. After all, Esras went up against his family too. But down the road, I could see where it could make for some ugly lovers' quarrels. Not to mention, awkward holidays.

There was also the fact that the fae age differently. While that seems to be the case for veil witches too, the feeling I get is that at some future point I'd be an old lady while Esras would remain, at most, middle-aged.

But the deciding factor was that people were already talking about whether Esras might be chosen for king. If that happened, it was speculated that he'd be expected to take an Unseelie bride as his queen. Esras said he wasn't interested in any of that, but I got one of those little psychic pings when thinking about it. I could see Esras making a great king, and I didn't want to be the one standing in his way, or in the way of what might be best for Faerie.

All of this might be a long way of saying that I freaked out once again when it came to commitment. I'm truly a mess on that score. But, hey, so far I've dated a necromancer, a changeling and a guy from Faerie. Needless to say, my love life has been complicated.

The music swells again, this time to signal that the guests of honor have all taken their seats. It's time to get this show on the road. All of us stare at Cade and Dabria, who now stand upon the altar, where a fae priestess will soon perform the ceremony.

Dabria looks radiant in her flowing silk gown, and Cade looks pretty dapper too in his new dark blue tunic. It too is made of the finest fabrics, the front brocaded with silver and gold. Upon his chest, he wears the medal bestowed upon him for the bravery he showed on behalf of the rebel cause. Way to go, Scamper. You really did end up being a hero, and it might well be that you'll be remembered in children's books.

Suddenly, a shadow falls over the crowd as something blocks out the sun. We all look up as massive scalloped wings push a breeze back down at us, and a long serpentine tail glides gracefully by.

Autumn gasps and grabs hold of my arm again. "They have dragons here?"

I smile and nod, but keep my eyes on the sky. After all, in the realm of Faerie, seeing a dragon is thought to be a very good omen. And I'm the one who set the dragon free.

EPILOGUE

It's a beautiful, crisp and clear day as I get off the bus and walk through Carytown on my way to Grimoire. I pull my jacket tight against a chilly breeze, but that's okay. We're heading into winter and it should be cold. Richmond doesn't get a lot of snow, but if we're lucky we'll get some soon. I've never felt more ready for winter. A real winter, with real ice and real snow. And, hey, maybe even a power outage or two. I'd be just fine with that too. That's what blankets and candles are for. Well, okay, kind of lying to myself there, but if my phone is fully charged I should be able to hack it for a couple of hours.

The bells on the front door jingle as I enter the old bookstore, where Maggie sits perched on a stool behind the counter. "Sorry I'm late," I say.

Why I say it, I'm not quite sure since I'm always late and Maggie never seems to care. In fact, it takes her a moment to look up from reading a beat up old volume she must have picked up on her rounds. I'm pretty sure she has the rest of Grimoire's books memorized.

"No worries, sweetie," she says. "Did you know that Leonardo Da Vinci was a witch?"

Despite the many things I've heard since living at the Cauldron and working at Grimoire, this one still stops me. "The painter?"

It's a ridiculous response, I realize. Who else could she possibly mean?

Maggie closes her book. "As well as inventor, mathematician, musician, architect and scientist."

"Just making sure we're talking about the same guy." I peel off my jacket, roll it into a ball and stuff it into one of the cabinets beneath the register.

"I didn't know either," Maggie says. "But it says here he may have been a speculomancer." She taps the worn leather cover of the book she was just reading.

"Huh?"

Maggie chuckles. "Mirror magic. Which, by the way, has long been considered to be veil witch magic. Leonardo even left a sketch behind called 'Witch Using a Magic Mirror.' The drawing's subject was a woman, of course, but we all know how Leonardo was when it came to women in his paintings."

"As in the Mona Lisa."

Maggie nods. "Exactly. So, let's assume the woman in the illustration was actually Leonardo Da Vinci, at least metaphorically. The book I was just reading described how Leonardo said she could use her magic mirror to see the future. Think about it. No one has ever figured out how he imagined so many inventions that didn't become part of reality until hundreds of years later. Airplanes, parachutes, the helicopter, the armored car, and so many others."

"Interesting theory. So, you're saying Leonardo could see the actual future, and it wasn't just that he had a powerful imagination."

"I'm sure it was both," Maggie says. "No one is asserting that Da Vinci wasn't a genius. Clearly, he was. Most witches display extraordinary intelligence levels, but I'm sure you know that."

My mind goes to recent antics involving Jerome and Bobby conjuring a Pocket Pixie and the spirit of a dead psychic, leaving me to silently ponder that point. Still, the idea of Leonardo Da Vinci having been a veil witch is beyond cool.

"By the way, I just made tea," Maggie says. "Pumpkin chai. It just seemed right for a chilly day like this. Oh, and there's brownies too. Help yourself, if you'd like."

The odds of me declining Maggie's offer of pumpkin chai and a brownie are about the same for me ever showing up on time. Right, never gonna happen. I go out back, fill a mug, snag a brownie, and pop back out front. I perch myself on a stool next to Maggie, prepared for a nice, mellow day spent watching an empty bookstore. Chances are, Maggie will soon depart for a date with one of her many middle-aged suitors. That's half the reason she hired me to begin with, not that I'm complaining. Basically, I get paid for sitting and stuffing my face.

Sure enough, Maggie's phone buzzes against the counter and she reads the text that just came in. She jumps up from her stool. "It's later than I thought. Tom's already at the restaurant."

I have no idea who Tom is, but I can pretty much bet that he and Maggie will be doing more than lunch, because Maggie soon has her coat on and is heading toward the door with a particularly lively bounce to her step.

She's just about to leave when suddenly she stops and turns around. She shakes her head and says, "Oh, my. I nearly forgot. There's someone out back in Special Collections. You should probably go and say hello."

I raise my eyebrows and wait for more. Generally, we don't bother those visiting the Special Collections room unless they ask for our help. After all, it's one of the few places where our fellow witches can sink their teeth into stacks of books dedicated to true magic.

"She said she knows you," Maggie says. "She seemed very nice. Okay, I should be back by four. Five at the latest."

The door closes behind her and Maggie bustles past the plate glass windows outside, while I sit there wondering who the hell could be out back in the Special Collections room. A chill runs through me that has nothing to do with the weather, as my heartbeat kicks up a notch. I tell myself I'm just being paranoid. Maggie said "she," so chances are it's either someone from the Cauldron or one of the local witches from the city coven. I mean, come on. It's not Vintain inhabiting Grayson or any other changeling. He's a done deal. I finish my brownie, take a last sip of my tea, and set off toward the room out back known to just the select few who are allowed access.

I enter the room to see a woman sitting at the old table in there. She's hunched over a book, with a stack of other books nearby. She has gray hair, and the lanyard of her reading glasses rests on the shoulders of her cardigan sweater. Apparently, she's too engrossed in her reading to have heard me come in.

I clear my throat and wait for her to look up. When she does, my heart nearly stops. Until this moment, I've assumed I'd never see her again. In fact, I've assumed that she never truly existed, along with the place where we met.

Beatrice's eyes meet mine and she smiles. "Oh, Cassie, there you are. It's so nice to see you again."

I open my mouth to speak, but no words come out as images flash through my mind. Riding in Grayson's sleek Jaguar. Parking in what looked to be an abandoned lot. Entering a building that just appeared out of nowhere to meet the same woman I'm now facing.

"I realize it's a little abrupt, just dropping in like this," Beatrice says. "But I've been meaning to ask. Have you given any more thought to working with us at the Shadow Order?"

Author Note

Thank you so much to all of you who have stayed with me through this series, reading various drafts and encouraging me to keep going when, at first, I wasn't sure how my version of Faerie lore would go over. I've loved writing these books, and your assistance and repeated reassurances have meant everything. I'd like to extend a very special thank you to those of you on the "beta-reading" team for offering your astute observations and eagle eyes! With that in mind, a most heartfelt thank you to Carmen Repsold, Tammy Baker, Jennifer Mantura, Deborah MacArthur, Marja Coons-Torn, Patti and Patrick Winters, Rachel Karfit, Lacey Lane, Lori Kis, Susan Warr, Andrea van der Westhuizen, Diane Changala, Ed Carr, Tamara Ingram, Tina Fulkerson, Vicki McCreary, Kim Brown, Amelia Donna Rose, Victoria McCreary, Deborah Smith, Maria Myrback, Bonnie Ellis, Jennifer Ryan, Cindy Love and Tisha. Thank you so much! You guys are fantastic readers and I truly appreciate your time and efforts. Many thanks also to Kim, Darja and Milo at Deranged Doctor Design for creating such stunning book covers.

About J. S. Malcom

J. S. Malcom is the author of the Realm Watchers urban fantasy series, of which Autumn Winters is just the beginning. J. S. lives in Richmond, Virginia, a town full of history and ghosts (not to mention, many other supernatural creatures, including Autumn and Cassie).

CPSIA information can be obtained
at www.ICGtesting.com
Printed in the USA
LVHW091151290920
667393LV00002B/766